CW01496638

# Escape To Cadrius

## Life and Philosophy in a Distant Future

Larry Haley

www.cadrius.com

For permissions:
https://cadrius.com/contact.html

Hardcover edition
ISBN 978-1-0882-9516-8

Library of Congress Control Number: 2023919769

# Table of Contents

# Chapter 1

## Escape

2092 CE

Savannah is in the market selecting meat for the meal she will prepare later.

A market worker, noticing the dull gray outfit with a black stripe down the side, asks her, "Who do you belong to?"

She hesitates, suppressing the emotions triggered by the question. Destiny is a short distance away selecting a sugar coated pastry. She stands tall, her head held high. Frowning, Savannah looks toward Destiny and says, "I belong to her."

***

Later, Destiny and her mother are sitting in the dining room drinking tea. Destiny is a young woman of about eighteen, with an air of wealth and entitlement, like her mother. She has rich, brown skin and a head full of tight, coily black hair that falls to her mid-back in thick, voluminous waves, often styled in an elaborate manner. Destiny is dressed to the nines, in luxurious designer clothes and expensive jewelry.

Destiny says, "Mom, I saw a video about poverty and violence in the slums. Why doesn't Zilnik do anything about it?"

"Zilnik is not at fault. Those people created their own situation. And he has people at the Isendul University studying the problem."

"Haven't they been studying the problem for years? Why don't they ever find a solution? Or at least try *something.*"

"Dear, you shouldn't be worrying about it. That is only in the slums, it doesn't affect us here in the Golden zone."

\*\*\*

Later, Savannah is working in the kitchen. Savannah is a servant girl about nineteen, the same age as Destiny. Savannah is a petite young woman with striking brown eyes that stand out against her creamy white complexion. She has long, wavy blonde hair that cascades down her back in gentle waves. Her features are delicate and ethereal, with a small nose. Destiny's family bought her when she was only a child, to be a playmate for Destiny. She hated the gray uniform she had to wear, it didn't go well with her white skin. She dreamed of being able to wear a beautiful dress. When they were younger, sometimes Destiny would dress up Savannah in Destiny's clothes, like she was dressing a toy doll. It stopped when Savannah began to look better in the clothes than Destiny.

The family treated her well, physically, but never having freedom to choose what one wears, where one goes, and never being able to say what you feel for fear of punishment; it was a kind of abuse. But Zondus society didn't recognize it as abuse if it happened to a slave.

Suddenly, Savannah hears a commotion in the dining room, she goes to see what is happening. Destiny's father says, "I'm sorry, I was just talking to my colleague. I thought the robot was far enough down the hall, I didn't think it could hear me."

Destiny's mother says, "You didn't think a robot could hear you? You thought you could just tell a co-worker that Zilnik is a tyrant and should be replaced? And you thought nothing would happen? What will we do? The police will arrest you!"

Destiny comes from another room. She says to her parents, "What's wrong? Why are you yelling?"

Destiny's mother says, "Your father discovered Zilnik has been lying about Cadrius." Her mother looks at him, "He thought it would be a good idea to tell a coworker that he thinks Zilnik is a tyrant."

Destiny gasps. Her mother continues, almost In tears, "I'm afraid the police are going to take him!"

Just then two cleaning robots stop their work and reboot. Destiny's father says to her, "They are going to take us. Here is my crypto drive." He places it on a string around her neck. He says, "They will probably make you leave the house. Listen to me, Cadrius is safe, Zilnik has been lying about it. Try to escape."

"No, you may have time to escape with me!"

The robot's front display changes, it says they are now operating for the police.

The robots quickly move and grab Destiny's parents by the arms. They both scream, "No!"

Destiny's father yells, "Why are you taking my wife?"

The robot says, "She is assumed to be a collaborator."

Just then, the front door opens and two larger police robots enter. They have special arms for immobilizing people. They take both of Destiny's parents, screaming.

Destiny yells, "Mother!" Her mother looks back as they take her away.

Destiny stands in shock. She turns to one of the cleaning robots that is still under police control and ask, "What will you do with me?"

The robot replies, "We don't have orders for you. But the house has been seized by the government. You have ten minutes to gather belongings and get out. You will have to leave the Golden zone, you are no longer in a favored family."

Savannah says, "What will we do?"

Destiny, breathing heavy with fear, almost crying, says, "I don't know." She thinks for a few seconds, "It's dangerous outside the Golden zone. Go to the kitchen and put some food in a bag. We're going to try to escape the city, Hurry! Get enough for at least two days."

Savannah, with a frown, goes to get the food. Destiny goes to her room and gets a bag with some things to do her hair and makeup.

They go out the front door past police robots. Destiny turns around and looks at the house. She whispers to herself, "I wonder if I will ever see the house again."

Savannah lugs two heavy bags.

They start walking to the gate of the Golden Zone. The neighbors across the street are staring at them. Destiny is embarrassed, the neighbors know what has happened. She knows not to expect any help from them. They will probably laugh about the plight of the traitors when they have dinner with their family. They will say they deserve what they get, and good riddance to those who don't support Zilnik.

Savannah asks, "Where will we go?"

Destiny says, "We'll go to Cadrius."

"What? There is no way we can make it there."

"Shut up! It's only forty kilometers."

***

Magnus is age twenty. He is tall, broad-shouldered with a commanding presence. He has a rich, dark complexion, brown hair, chiseled features and expressive brown eyes.

Magnus is with his family in the slums. They are in their shack made from scavenged boards with a roof made of old sheet metal. Scraps of foam insulate the roof and walls. Magnus' father yells at him, "It's time for you to get out! There is not enough food for all of us! Get out!"

"But where will I go?"

"I don't care, you will find something!"

Magnus' mother says, "Please don't make him go!"

Magnus puts his belongings in a bag and leaves.

***

Magnus, on the street, calls his cousin Lennon, "Hey, my dad kicked me out. He said there's not enough food for us all."

Lennon, on the phone, says, "I can't help you, I'm not in Zondus."

"What do you mean? Where are you?"

"I'm in Cadrius."

"What? Are you okay? Did they kidnap you?"

"No, it's not like that. The Cadrians are good people. They are treating me well and there is plenty to eat here. Zilnik has been lying to us, Cadrians are not evil."

"What? But I've heard my whole life how evil they are. It's not true? It's safe there and there is food?"

"Yes. You should come if you have been kicked out. It's only two days walk across Tarphit."

Magnus thinks. He says, "Okay, I will try to come."

He ends the call and starts walking. After a few blocks, he sees his friend Vincent, also about age twenty, lying on the side of the street.

Vincent has a deep, caramel complexion and closely cropped, curly black hair. His features are sharp and angular, with a strong jawline and piercing brown eyes.

Magnus says to Vincent, "Are you okay? Why are you out here?"

Vincent says, "I left home, there is not enough food."

"I'm going to Cadrius. My cousin Lennon says there is food there and Zilnik has been lying to us about it. Come with me."

"Okay, I will go with you. If I stay here I'll die."

***

Alissa and River, both age twenty five, are talking outside the gate of Glendor, a small city at the edge of Isendul.

Alissa is a slight, pale young woman, somewhat shorter than average. She has piercing blue eyes that seem to see straight through you and straight, jet-black hair that falls in a straight line to her mid-back. Her features are delicate and precise, with high, defined cheekbones. Alissa always dresses in simple, tailored clothing that emphasizes her intellect.

River is shorter than average with a slender, willowy build. River has a clear, luminous complexion and striking eyes that are an enigmatic shade of gray. River's gender is difficult to distinguish and they have hair that is long, wavy, and a bright, shining silver that seems to change colors in different light.

River says, "The Glendor AI says the waiting list is too long. The fastest way is to go to Cadrius and take their training."

"Cadrius? The spirit of my great grandmother foretold that I would go to Cadrius. But my family attends the Church of Zilnik, contact with Cadrians is against their teachings. If they discover I have gone to Cadrius, they will disown me."

"I think you should be done with them; they are not good for you."

Alissa thinks. She says, "I will admit Glendor has a better way of life. They are honest, they have always treated us well. It's a better place to live."

"Come with me. I love you and I need you with me."

"Alright, I will go with you."

***

Destiny and Savannah walk down the street. The homes in the Golden Zone are nice but gaudy, meant to impress with size. The street is clean and well landscaped. They pass a park for children to play in. There is a nearby shopping mall with an ice cream shop. A perfect place to live. Destiny and Savannah walk past these things for the last time.

They walk out of the Golden Zone, the gated area for the elite members of Isendul, the capital of Zondus. Outside of the Golden Zone, it is all slums.

The slums are dirty, trash everywhere, overcrowded, buildings falling apart. The slums are dangerous, gangs are in control. Destiny looks around, feeling unsafe. The gangs have setup checkpoints and require a fee to pass. They walk up. Destiny pays and they keep walking.

A stranger says to them, "You look like you are from the Golden zone. We don't see many people from there."

Destiny says nothing, walks faster, Savannah follows.

An older man with a long beard sitting on the ground yells at them, "Hey, what you got in those bags?" He gets up and runs after them. Destiny and Savannah run. They are able to escape because the man is older and out of shape. When they are safe they stop to catch their breath. Destiny is shaking with fear.

They walk through the slums until they reach the edge of Isendul. Before them is the wasteland of Tarphit, a plain of dry orange and white clay with occasional gullies that feed into small canyons. They embark across Tarphit.

Destiny's phone says, "You have no reason to enter Tarphit, there is nothing there. Only Cadrius is ahead, and there is nothing for you there. Cadrians will kill you."

Destiny throws down the phone. Then she takes the tracking device off Savannah's ankle and throws it down.

Savannah says, "What are you doing? It's illegal to be without those devices."

Destiny says, "Shut up. Let's go."

*** 

After about four hours of walking, they stop to eat and rest. Destiny looks back toward Isendul, "Look, someone is coming this way." There are two people about a hundred meters away.

Destiny says, "It looks like some poor commoners."

The strangers approach. It is two men, one says, "Are you going to Cadrius too?"

"Yes" says Destiny.

"May we walk with you? I'm Magnus and this is Vincent."

"Hello." says Vincent.

"I'm Destiny."

Magnus and Vincent are aware of the gray uniform Savannah wears. Magnus asks her, "What is your name?"

Destiny says, "Don't talk to her. Her name is Savannah, she's my indentured servant. She was found in the slums, her family was deeply in debt. My family purchased her from a dealer and rescued her."

Savannah looks ashamed to be talked about this way with strangers.

Magnus says, "She doesn't look like she's been rescued." Magnus smiles at Savannah. She smiles but quickly looks down.

Vincent looks at the food, "I haven't eaten in two days."

Destiny somewhat reluctantly hands hims a food package. She is thinking the supplies are limited and they belong to her.

"Thank you. Thank you." Vincent says. He sits down, opens it and eats ravenously. He says, "I'm leaving Zondus because there's not enough to eat."

He takes another bite. He says, "I can see from the way you're dressed you're from an elite family. Why are you going to Cadrius? It can't be because you are running out of food."

Destiny says, "My father learned Zilnik has been telling lies about Cadrius. My parents were arrested for treason. They seized our house."

Later, Savannah asks Destiny, "What do you think will happen when we get to Cadrius? Will they let us stay? Zilnik says Cadrians are evil. I'm afraid."

Destiny says, "Father discovered Zilnik is lying, that's why the police took him away. They were afraid he would talk."

"What if your father was wrong? Will you trade me to the Cadrians to save yourself?"

"Be quiet."

Savannah looks like she will cry.

Magnus stares at Savannah, looking so vulnerable and afraid, but also beautiful. Magnus says, "I have a cousin that went to Cadrius two weeks ago. I talked to him by phone and he said that he was welcomed and there is plenty of food."

Savannah says, "Really? It is safe?"

"Yes." says Magnus.

Savannah looks relieved. She looks at him with big eyes and says, "Thank you." He looks into her eyes, she smiles shyly and looks away.

Destiny says, "I have heard people in Cadrius talk strangely, they don't say 'he' or 'she', they say something else."

Magnus says, "They say 'e' instead of those. I have seen videos, they sound strange, but you can understand them."

When they are done, Destiny says to Savannah, "Pack up the supplies, we are going."

Savannah packs the bag.

Magnus says, "Let me carry that for you."

Destiny says, "It's her job, she wants to do it."

Savannah says nothing, standing frozen.

Magnus shakes his head and says, "That's what you tell yourself to make yourself feel better about how you treat her."

Destiny gives him a look, then walks away muttering profanities.

Magnus reaches out and takes the bag from Savannah. She whispers, "Thank you."

They all begin walking to Cadrius again. The sky is clear and the sun is hot. There is no shade anywhere. They come to a gully about eight meters deep. The sides are steep enough they have to go down carefully to avoid a fall. Going up the other side is even more difficult.

Later, the sun is going down. They stop for the night. Vincent has a lantern, he sets it up as it gets dark and everyone sits in a circle around it, their faces aglow from its light.

Soon they are all tired and ready for sleep.

The next morning, as the sky begins to glow, they eat the last of the food. Destiny says to Savannah, "I wonder if it was a mistake to share our food. Those guys eat a lot."

Vincent looks around as though someone could attack at any moment. He says, "I think we should get going." They start walking.

They pass by some metal equipment and some wood that looks like it could have once been a house. Vincent says, "My grandfather told me Tarphit was once productive farm land. He used to live here."

Destiny says, "How can that be? There is nothing here now."

"The land was overworked and the topsoil eroded away. It was because of short sighted instructions from the government. They wanted to maximize yield in the short term, they didn't care about the future. The farmers wouldn't make enough money to live unless they produced their quota."

Destiny feels the weight of losing her parents, her home, the unknown of what is to come. She looks out solemnly across the landscape, the blue sky, the orange ground, beautiful and desolate.

# Chapter 2

## Crossing Over

At mid day, they come out of a gully onto a plain of clay. Destiny says, "Look! What is it?" Ahead of them is a line of green on the horizon.

Vincent says, "It's a forest! It must be the border of Cadrius!" He pauses, then says, "Tarphit used to be green like that."

The four all start walking faster. Soon they are at the edge of the forest. They see a marker. Magnus says, "It *is* the border!" They walk into the forest.

The bright sun filters through the canopy of the green forest, leaves glow where the sunlight falls on them. The tree trunks, some large, some bent, some are vine covered. There are mats of soft green moss, and mushrooms.

Destiny says, "Some of these trees look so old. What if they could talk about the things that have seen?"

After they go about twenty meters into the forest, they hear a voice, it says, "Greetings, welcome to Cadrius."

Destiny says, "Where did that come from? I wasn't serious about the trees talking."

Vincent says, "It's coming from a box attached to that tree."

The box says, "Greetings. This video feed may be monitored by humans. Why have you come to Cadrius?"

Vincent moves closer and says, "We're from Zondus. We had to leave our homes because there are no jobs. We are hungry and seek refuge."

The box says, "All are welcome in Cadrius. There is a supply station four hundred meters to the southwest. The monitors on the others trees will guide you."

"Thank you." says Vincent.

They walk to the supply station. The station is operated by a robot. The robot says, "Greetings. Welcome to Cadrius. There is food and drink here. I can also provide first aid and clothing if needed." They walk in and look around. There is fresh made bread in a basket and other food packaged in glass jars.

Magnus asks, "Why is everything in jars? Plastic wrap would be cheaper."

The robot says, "Cadrians don't use throw away packaging. We use glass instead."

They all select whatever looks good to them and eat gladly.

Vincent says to the robot, "We seek refuge in Cadrius because of the economic conditions in Zondus. Will Cadrius accept us?"

"Economic refugees will be accepted for a period up to one year for rehabilitation and training."

Vincent says, "One year? What happens after that?"

"You will be required to return to Zondus. You will have the opportunity to settle in an area prepared by Cadrius."

The robot looks at Savannah and says, "You wear the Zondus clothing of an indentured servant. Do you have a master?"

Savannah gestures and says quietly, "Destiny is my master."

The robot says to Savannah, "The country of Cadrius does not recognize indentured servitude. You are a free person here."

Savannah's eyes get big and she lets out a squeal of excitement. Destiny says, "What?! Savannah belongs to me! You can't take her without compensation!"

The robot says, "Your claim is invalid here."

Destiny says to Savannah, "Don't get any ideas, Savannah, you will do as you are told."

Savannah looks at Destiny and says in words that burn, "You have told me what to do for long enough. Maybe we had some fun when we were small, but then you grew up and became a 'master' and made me clean your toilets and you treated me like nothing."

Savannah turns around to walk away. Destiny draws her hand back and takes a step toward Savannah as though she will hit her, but the robot grabs her wrist, she pulls with a groan. The robot says, "Violence is not allowed here."

After they calm down and finish eating, another robot with wheels for rough terrain leads them a few kilometers down a trail. Savannah walks at the front, behind the robot; Destiny walks last, solemnly, behind all the others.

Magnus says to Savannah as they walk, "I'm glad you are free now."

Savannah says, "It's so wonderful, and so… unexpected, I'm still processing it. Cadrius has already given me the gift of freedom. Before, I just did what Destiny told me to do. Now, I can make my own decisions. Maybe they will let me work, then I can have my own money. I can buy what I want and do what I want."

Magnus says, "I hope all of that comes true for you."

The robot says to the group, "We will soon arrive at Navora. The city is prepared to receive refugees. There are residents of Navora who wish to greet you and honor you for your courage in leaving your homeland. They have been watching your approach through the surveillance cameras. After you arrive, there will be a medical exam, then you will be shown to apartments. Your movements will be limited until your psychological evaluations are complete. Then your training will begin. If at any point you do not wish to stay in Cadrius, you will be allow to return to Zondus." They all look at each other. No one wants to return to Zondus.

# Chapter 3

## Arrival

They continue walking and soon the trail converges with another trail and becomes a paved walkway.

Soon they are emerging from the forest and the four stop and stare at the size of the building in front of them. It is about a kilometer wide and about seventy meters high. Its architecture is beautiful, the exterior walls are not simple vertical walls but carved stone terraces, balconies, and layers of projections.

The walkway passes through an orchard of fruit trees on one side of Navora. The orchard is in bloom. The path leads to the entrance of the city, ahead. About a hundred people are gathered on each side of the entrance to cheer for new refugees. More are watching from balconies on the building.

They shout to them…

"Welcome!"

"We honor you!"

"You are miracles of creation!"

"Come, be a part of our city!"

They are astonished and they can't help but smile at such goodwill.

Some say to Savannah, "Congratulation on your freedom!" "Freedom freedom freedom!"

They enter a door and air blows them. The robot explains, "The air is to decontaminate you of insects."

After they pass through another the door, an AI eye on the wall identifies a flying insect and zaps it with a laser, creating a small puff of smoke.

They are separated into individual rooms and given a medical evaluation by robots and doctors checking for diseases, parasites, and malnutrition. They are asked if they need any special food or medication. Next, they enter a dining hall and are given food.

Then they are given watchers, a small device that sits on their shoulder that monitors their activities. They are told they must wear them constantly. Only AIs will monitor, not humans.

After the evaluation, they are escorted by robots to apartments.

Vincent enters and says to the robot, "Wow, this is way better than the slum where I lived in Zondus."

The robot says, "Greetings, allow me to show you the apartment." The robot is the type that balances on two wheels. It is 130 centimeters high and has a small head that is really just a camera. It has two arms with three fingers at the end.

The robot moves and points, "On this side of the room are live plants, which I maintained. Here is a video screen for entertainment. And there is a tablet with internet, you can use it for video calls. Here is a balcony with a view."

Vincent is speechless. He has only seen videos of such luxuries.

"Here is the kitchen, I can prepare a full meal or I can do only prep and clean-up if you wish to do your own cooking."

"Really? I just ask and you will prepare food?"

"Yes."

"Then I would like a steak and baked potato. And apple pie for dessert."

"Acknowledged. I estimate it will be ready in one hour." The robot rolls away.

Vincent says to himself, "This is amazing."

Later, when the food is ready and he sits down to eat, he takes a bite of the meat, he says, "Mmm, this is wonderful. It's been a long time since I had real meat. It's hard to get in Zondus."

"It is good to know you enjoy it sir. But I must disclose that is factory grown meat. It is not from a cow."

"Really? It tastes so real."

"In Cadrius, animals are not killed for food. We use technology to grow animal cells to form meat."

"It works really well."

\*\*\*

The robot in Destiny's room says, "An AI from the government of Cadrius will now speak to you."

"Hello. I am an agent of the government of Cadrius. I will need to ask you some questions so you may be registered as a resident of Navora."

"Alright." she says.

"Please state you full name."

"Destiny Gahoni."

"Why have you come to Cadrius?"

"My parents were taken by the state police. They feared he would expose Zilnik. My father told me to come to Cadrius, he feared for my safety."

"So you are the child of a political dissident. Do you intent to comply with the ethics of Cadrius?"

"I do."

"I need to take biometric data for identification." The robot extends its hands forward. "Please place all of your finger around the edge of my hands, the sides contain a ring of fingerprint sensors."

Destiny complies.

The robot then says, "My eye cameras also act as retinal scanners, please move close and look into them."

Destiny does so.

The robot says, "Welcome to Cadrius. You will be allowed to stay one year for training. Then you will be required to return to Zondus."

"Is there any way I can stay longer?"

"No. The population level in Cadrius is controlled and at its maximum. If the population limit does not increase, you will be required to leave Cadrius in one year. Second, The policy of Cadrius is that you must return to Zondus to work for change."

"Work for change? What can I do?"

"Part of your education will include methods you can use to influence the politics of Zondus."

The robot continues, "You have been provided with a financial account in the Cadrius system. Do you have any assets from Zondus?"

Destiny hesitates then says, "I have some crypto."

"You may use the assets to fund your account."

Destiny plugs the drive into a port on the robot. The robot says, "The value is one hundred seventy percent of the endowed level. You may invest it and use the proceeds to meet your financial needs perpetually. Would you like to invest the assets now?"

"Yes."

\*\*\*

In Savannah's quarters, she has been asked the same questions. The robot says, "Welcome to Cadrius. You have been provided with a financial account in the Cadrius system. Do you have any assets from Zondus?"

Savannah looks down, "No, I have nothing."

"Since you crossed the border of Cadrius, citizens have monitored your progress. They observed your reaction when you learned you were free. Many were moved with compassion for you and donated funds for you."

"They donated funds for me?"

"Yes, you have received the endowment level. You can invest the funds and receive an income that will meet all your needs."

Savannah says, "I am so thankful." She wipes away tears.

\*\*\*

In Vincent's room, the robot says, "I will now ask some questions about your history. Have you ever been involved in acts of violence?"

Vincent pauses, then looks down and says, "Where I lived in Isendul, there were no jobs because of the robots. To live, my only choice was to work for the gangs. I stole for them."

"Did you ever injure anyone?"

"Yes. Sometimes I had to."

The robot says without emotion, "You will require treatment for violence."

"What does that mean?"

"You will be given additional training and testing for empathy, equality and non-violence. You indicate that your

21

use of violence was not chosen, that should make your training faster. However, you will need to remain in these quarters until you are qualified to move about the city, then there will be probation."

"How long is my sentence?"

"It is not a sentence, there is no set time period, your progress determines the time."

"I will cooperate. It is a great opportunity I have in being here. But what would happen if I don't pass all the training? Can I stay longer for additional training?"

The robot says, "No. We have to make room for new refugees. You will have to return when your time is completed. Do not worry, you will have every opportunity to successfully complete the training. However, if you fail your training, you will not be allowed to go to a Cadrius sponsored outpost. You will be returned to Isendul."

"You mean I would have to return to the slums of Isendul?"

"Yes."

*** 

In Savannah's quarters, the robot asks, "Would you like a change of clothes? There are fresh clothes in the bedroom closet."

Savannah says, "Yes, I would be glad to get rids of these horrid slave clothes!"

She goes and finds new clothes of the Cadrian style. Black tee shirt and leggings, a colored tunic. She put them on and throws the old slave clothes across the room.

Savannah finally has time to relax. She looks out the window. She says to herself, "This place is so wonderful.

But it will only lasts a year. Then I will be returned to Zondus. And slavery." She looks somber.

# Chapter 4

## Courage

The refugees are all given study assignments reading and watching videos in their apartments. When Cadrian educators created the videos, they used interesting and articulate speakers.

The refugees learn about the history of Cadrius and its philosophy. They learn about customs and cultural traditions. They learn Zondian history they have never heard, from Zondian books and news that were banned.

In addition to the videos, they have conversations with people and AIs about the subjects. Mentors are assigned to the students.

Destiny is in her room. The robot says, "Your mentor, Eli, would like to meet you."

Destiny opens the door. Eli says with enthusiasm, "Hello Destiny, I am Eli, it is a pleasure to meet you!" He bows with a moderate bow, a tradition of Cadrians who do not commonly shake hands.

Eli, about age forty, wears a common Cadrian outfit of black shirt and pants covered with a red tunic. Eli is a jovial man of average height. He has warm, chestnut-colored skin and a full, bushy dark beard that frames his smiling face. His eyes are bright and crinkled at the corners, as if he's always ready to laugh. Eli's hair is curly and dark.

Eli says, "I hope that you are well and your accommodations meet your needs."

Destiny says, "The room is fine." But she sounds somber as she says it.

"What troubles you, my dear?"

"My parents are in Zondus. My father discovered the propaganda ministry in Zondus has been lying to us. My father said some things to a coworker against Zilnik. A robot overheard and my parents were taken by the Zondian police. It's a crime to criticize Zilnik in any way. I am afraid they will be executed." Destiny cries.

"Oh my dear, I am so sorry. That is a tragedy."

He hugs her. Eli cries with her.

Eli says, "Your parents should not have to die for speaking out."

Eli continues, "Being punished for speaking is a foreign concept to us. In Cadrius, we can speak what we believe. We can question authority, but we do so politely. How else can society improve if we don't question things?"

Destiny looks like she is thinking, then she says,"You mean, in Cadrius I can speak against Zilnik?"

"Yes. If you dislike what e has done, you are free to say so."

Destiny looks angry, thinking about the situation of her parents. Eli says, "If you need to yell about it, you may do so."

Destiny screams, "I hate Zilnik! I hate him with all my heart!"

Eli says, "Get it out. You can describe how you feel."

"I am angry. I am angry at what he has done to my family!"

"Very good. Very good. It is good to see you accurately express how you feel. Many from Zondus have difficulty expressing their feelings."

Eli says, "Did you have any other family members in Zondus?"

Destiny thinks and says, "There was Savannah."

"But e was a slave, not part of your family, is that correct?"

"Yes, but she was like family to me."

Eli says, "I wonder if Savannah felt that way."

***

Later, Melina, another mentor, comes to Destiny's apartment. Melina is twenty eight. Melina is a petite young woman of average height. She has creamy skin and big, soulful brown eyes that seem to see straight into your heart. Melina's hair is straight chestnut brown that frames her delicate features. Melina moves with quiet strength, confidence and grace. She is a quiet, stoic person, raised from birth in Cadrian society. She is dressed in Cadrian clothes consisting a burgundy tunic with black tights.

Destiny opens the door and Melina bows and says, "Hello, I am Melina, it's nice to meet you. I'm glad you found your way to Navora."

"Thank you."

When Melina speaks, she shows a certain calmness. Whether something good or bad is spoken of, she is prepared for either. She says, "I understand your parents have been taken into custody for political reasons."

"Yes. I don't know if they will be executed." She wipes a tear.

Melina pauses, then says, "I want you to know we are here to support you. This is a time of transition for you and your family. You are in a new country, new circumstances. It is completely normal to feel the way you do. Let me offer this encouragement, you have the ability to endure the weight of these circumstances. You have the ability to recover, more than you may think. And we will be here to help you."

Destiny says, "Thank you. The hardest part is not knowing."

Melina says, "Courage means to endure pain when we must. The pain of uncertainty. The symbol we use for courage is the column. It symbolizes that we can bear the challenges that come to us. We have a phrase: 'When the weight comes down.' It means it is a time when we need to bear the weight of a great challenge."

*** 

Later, The robot in Destiny's room says, "I have a question. Do you have a partner? Or, as you may say, a spouse?"

"Oh, no, I don't."

"If you would like one, I can assist with matching you."

Destiny looks surprised, "I suppose, someday."

The robot says, "Cadrius policy is that people should not be lonely. But it is your choice."

*** 

A few days later, Eli meets Destiny at a food establishment where people often gather and have

27

discussions. It includes an indoor playground with large windows so that customers can watch children.

Destiny says to Eli, "I have been working on the concept of equality. I think I understand now that all people are equal."

Eli says, "Very good. I have some exercises for you. Remember a few days ago, when you were angry, you said how much you hated Zilnik?"

"Yes."

"I would challenge you to purge hate from yourself as much as you can."

"You mean, control myself and don't say I hate him?"

"It's not about controlling what you say. It's about your motivation, what you feel inside. If you don't do the hating, you won't do the saying."

"You mean actually try not to hate him?" Destiny shakes her head. "That is too far of a stretch for me."

"Alright, alright. Then I have another exercise for you. I'm going to name some people and you tell me if they are more or less important than yourself."

"Okay."

"Your parents."

"Equal."

"Magnus"

She thinks a second, "Equal."

"Savannah"

Destiny looks questioning, "I have been working on this. It is difficult for me to think of her as an equal, for so many years I saw her as an inferior. But each day I tell myself she is my equal."

Eli says, "That's acceptable."

Eli watches the children, he smiles then laughs. Eli says, more serious now, "I have one more for you. Perhaps it would be possible to begin thinking of Zilnik as an equal."

Destiny says, "I cannot think of him as an equal! He thinks he is above everyone!" Destiny grits her teeth. "But he is not. He is the worst!"

Eli says, "Alright. Calm down. E is guilty of crimes, but e is still a human being."

Destiny says, "Him and his policies are responsible for my parents' imprisonment. I cannot forgive him!" Destiny pauses for a moment, then says, "What would you do if you had him here in Navora? Like, if you were able to capture him?"

Eli says, "E would be taken into custody, e would be confined to quarters and we would work on teaching em Cadrian values."

Destiny says, "So he would get a life as good as I have?"

"Well, yes."

"And how long would he be confined?"

"Well, there would not be a fixed time, I would expect someone like em to require years of treatment."

"And then he could be released? How is that fair to all those he oppressed?"

Eli says, "Remember that our goal is not retribution. We only want to teach people to live their own life in a community, and to make the community better."

"How could Zilnik make any community better?"

"We believe most people can change with training and become a positive member of a community."

***

Vincent studies in his apartment. In addition to equality and justice, he studies anger management. There are questionnaires about his anger responses. He is shown videos of anger provoking situations and he has discussions with AIs on how to deal with the situations or reframe them in his mind.

Vincent passes his studies of anger management and is released from confinement.

***

The next day, Eli escorts Destiny, Savannah, Magnus, and Vincent into a meeting room where two other people are waiting.

Savannah carries herself with a new sense of confidence dressed in bold, vibrant colors. Destiny looks at her with disdain.

Eli says, "I would like you to meet River and Alissa." They stand and everyone bows.

Eli says, "River and Alissa are also from Zondus. They are partners. They will be learning along with you and will be returning to Zondus as you will."

Magnus asks River, "You came to Cadrius from Zondus?"

River says, "Yes, I was looking for a job and heard there was work in Glendor. We wanted to live there but they require training. The waiting list for training in Glendor was many months, we could start faster by coming to Cadrius. And we knew it was safe here too."

Magnus asks, "What is Glendor?"

River says, "Glendor is a Cadrian trading center just outside Isendul in Zondus. Refugees trained in Cadrius came and cleared an area of abandoned slums and began building a city. The government ignores Glendor as long as it doesn't cause problems for the government."

Alissa says, "There is a thriving market in Glendor, many people from the Isendul slums come to buy there. Many things that are hard to get in Zondus are available. It has the best variety and the best prices. But most of all, the sellers of Glendor are honest, they do not cheat anyone, their products are of the highest quality. Because of that they have gained a reputation. The entrance to the market is a gate that is well known as a place of safety because the gangs don't control beyond it."

River says, "Glendor also has the best hospital in Zondus."

Eli says, "I have someone else I would like you all to meet. I would ask you to limit your reaction to eir appearance."

The five look at each other, expecting someone that has some kind of injury.

Eli brings in someone. The six eyes grow large and some of their mouths are open wide, but they quickly compose themselves. They wonder, is this a person or … a cat? E stands about 110 centimeters high. E is covered with orange and white fur and has cat-like ears. E stands holding eir hands (paws?) in front of emself.

Eli says, "This is Catifur."

Catifur says, "Hello." in a rather high pitched voice.

They are surprised e can talk. Eli says, "Catifur was liberated from Zondus by some of our operatives. Catifur is the result of genetic experiments in Zondus. We call eir an enhanced cat, or e-cat. Experiments were done to em and later e was treated as a 'pet'."

Eli says, "I wanted you to meet Catifur because there are others like eir in Zondus. They are seen as less than a person and are being mistreated. Catifur has some things e would like to say."

Catifur says, "I want you to know that even though I look different, I have feelings. Those like me should not be treated as less than a person. Someday, you will return to Zondus. I ask you to do all you can to help those like me. If you can work to change attitudes, to bring awareness, or if you can have any influence to change the government, please do all you can. Thank you."

Vincent stands and says, "I see that you are beautiful and intelligent. And I see you as equal to us all. I will do all that I can to help the other e-cats."

Catifur goes up to him and takes his hand and rubs eir face against the back his hand. Vincent says, "That feels so good."

***

Later, Destiny asks Eli, "Does the principle of equality also apply to animals? Are animals as important as humans?"

"There is a school of thought that says they are. Because of that, exploitation of animals has been eliminated by Cadrius. We reserve habitat for wildlife between our cities. But there is a limit to how equal animals can be. When we walk across an outdoor field, inevitably we step on small creatures and kills some. If a wild animal were to threaten attack of a human, the animal would be stopped by a robot, by lethal force if necessary. The limits of our compassion are a matter of debate."

\*\*\*

Vincent exits the gate that leads to a field on the east side of Navora. It is his first time outdoors since coming to Navora. He walks about four hundred meters, until he is closer to the forest than the city. He takes a moment to look around at the trees, the sky, the grass. He looks all around, and thinks with a feeling of exhilaration that he is free, he is safe.

In a few minutes, Savannah approaches. She says to Vincent, "You look so happy."

"I have come to realize how unsafe I felt in Zondus. I lived my whole life surrounded by crime and abuse. And now, here, I realize I am safe." He looks around, "I know it sounds crazy, but this is the best day of my life."

Savannah smiles, "That is so wonderful, so beautiful!" She hugs him.

# Chapter 5

## Elevation

Magnus is in his apartment and speaks to the AI through the watcher on his shoulder, "I'm really having trouble with this concept of 'elevation'. In Zondus, my family yelled at me, told me I was no good, worthless, a waste of resources. But these lessons tell me that I am a miracle. It is new to me, and I am having trouble believing it."

The AI says, "Think for a moment of how humans are made. Each of your cells have many processes. You breathe, you metabolize, you heal, you think, you feel emotions, you remember, you move, you see, you hear. These are all miracles. You, and all people, are rare in the universe; you are valuable, irreplaceable, and unique."

The AI continues, "This is the greatest of the philosophies of Cadrius. To see human life as a miracle. This idea leads humans to think positively of others. It allows people to change the internal narratives that feed hate and envy, which can grow into offense and violence. Elevation removes the conditions that result in provocation and offense. It teaches people to respect the possessions of others, to be a good friend, and not to act with intent to harm."

Magnus says, "But will that not make people weak? People need some abuse to make them strong."

The AI says, "That is untrue. Research has found that uninjured people are stronger than those who are abused."

Magnus thinks, then says, "This is going to take time for me to absorb. What I learned my whole life up to this point was so different."

The AI says, "Take the time you need. Review the research if you have doubts. All that you are going through is expected and normal."

Magnus thinks. He sits and looks out the window.

***

In Savannah's quarters, Savannah asks the robot AI, "I know we have a limited time in Cadrius, and then we will have to return to Zondus. Are there any exceptions? Is there any way I can stay here?"

The robot says, "The population of Navora and Cadrius is controlled. Refugees must leave after training to make room for more refugees."

Savannah looks sad at the thought of being returned to slavery. Her lower lip quivers.

***

The next day, Eli is with Magnus in Bonasta Garden, an indoor garden with flowering plants, butterflies, and small trees.

On each side of the walkway are arrays of lush green plants of every kind. Some low, obscuring the ground. Some above one's head. At every level, color, dominated by green; every other color represented by flowers, bark, stem, or wing. Water, flowing, falling into pools. Butterflies, colors in motion, occasionally resting,

35

occasionally feeding. Bees, flying to each flowers, feeding on nectar. Small birds, tweeting, singing, some above in the trees, some on the ground, always out of reach. The whole scene, random, yet structured colors, motion, sounds, smells, textures.

There are tables arranged between plant groupings. Robots serve refreshments. Magnus says, "This place is beautiful. Look, there are butterflies!" He looks around in awe.

Eli says, "I thought you would like it, I come here often." Eli looks around with almost as much wonder as Magnus, even though he has been coming here for years.

Eli says, "There are numerous gardens throughout Navora. They all have unique themes and layouts."

Magnus says, "There is nothing like this in Zondus. I don't think anyone there cares enough to build something like this."

Eli says, "The attitude that we are all miracles of creation drives us to build such things. Both the butterfly and we ourselves are miracles."

Eli continues, "We believe peace grows between people when we focus on the positive, even miraculous aspects of humanity. It is our practice to see both the imperfections of humanity and to see humanity as a miracle. The sanctity of each of us. We call this practice *elevation*."

Magnus says, "How do you do this practice, of seeing other people as miracles?"

Eli says, "We focus on the commonalities humans share: we breath, our blood flows, we digest food, we are conscious, we sense, we feel, we think, we grow, we heal. All of these are evidence of the miracle that is life.

"We maintain awareness of things like the biology of life, our human abilities of consciousness, thinking, movement. Our ability to comprehend the world, galaxies, the universe. Would you agree that all of these things are miracles?"

"I have never thought about it, but yes, they are miracles."

Eli continues, "This way of seeing people affects our attitude toward others. It leads us to build a good community for everyone. That is why we designed spaces like this into Navora. It is a reason for the architecture and aesthetic of Navora and other Cadrian cities."

"I don't see the connection"

"The attitude of each person designing and operating the components of our community affect how they are designed and how the components operate. Each person contributes to their community in some way. If they have a negative attitude they will not put sufficient effort into the design of the components that make up their community. We believe society depends on the contributions by each individual. That is the reason we try to teach elevation to everyone.

"We avoid doing anything to harm society. We are told that in the absence of elevation, people have a tendency to think negatively of each other, which can result in resentment and anger toward others. Would you says this is true?"

Magnus says, "Certainly anger and resentment are the norm in Zondus, but I cannot say if the absence of elevation is the cause."

Eli says, "I don't know if anger is the human default, or if it is taught by culture. Or perhaps a third explanation, perhaps anger is an adaptation to a sick society."

Magnus looks around at the plants and butterflies. He says, "I think a place like this would soon be vandalized in Zondus."

Eli says, "Why would anyone vandalize a place like this?"

"Some people don't appreciate beautiful things. I think there are those with so much pain, they release it on anything people enjoy."

"I don't think we have people like that here. Are there not robots that record crimes?"

"Privacy is paramount in Zondus. Robots are trained to ignore crimes. And the authorities make little effort to investigate, outside the Golden Zone anyway."

Eli sighs and says, "Having a good life is not so difficult if your neighbors do not work against you. So many things are wrong in Zondus. Perhaps if we could teach elevation, Zondians would then respect people and their property."

Magnus puts his hand on his chin, but does not answer.

Eli says, "I have heard people sell illegal drugs in Zondus."

Magnus says, "It is true, many people work to produce and sell illegal drugs. Many lives are harmed by drugs."

Eli says, "In Cadrius, we direct our work efforts to making positive contributions to society. It is difficult for me to imagine doing work that harms others. Even if those people desire the thing that harms them."

Eli says, "I will be going now. I would like see you later at your apartment. And I would like to bring the others, if you agree."

Magnus says, "That will be fine."

***

Later, at Magnus' apartment, Eli and the others come in with greetings.

Eli says to the robot, "Please adjust the lighting."

The lights dim, except for a light shining straight down in the center of the room. There is gentle music, what some might call 'spa' music. The other teachers, Melina and Orla are there, and also Destiny, Savannah, Vincent, River and Alissa.

Magnus is curious about what will happen.

Eli says, "Magnus, please stand here in the light. All the others will circle around you. This is called 'The Raising' and is meant to be a blessing on you."

Eli gives everyone in the circle some cards. Eli, followed by the others, one-at-a-time stands in front of Magnus and reads from a card and looks Magnus in the eye. Eli begins, "Magnus, you are human like all of us. There is so much positive about you."

"You breath."

"You use your senses."

"Your blood flows."

"You digest food."

"You are conscious."

"You feel."

"You think."

"You grow."

"You heal."

"You are important."

"You are equally important as anyone."

"Your mind is capable of solving mysteries."

"You have unmeasured potential."

"You are capable of overcoming difficult challenges."

"You learn and discover."

"You thirst for knowledge."

"You have love and joy for life."

"You innovate."

"You create."

"You have the power to change the world."

"You are a flower in the garden of humanity."

"You are enough."

"You are worthy of love."

"There is no one exactly like you in all the world."

"You are a miracle of creation."

Magnus begins to cry. He says "I remember when my parents would belittle me and criticize my every move. I never met their expectations. And bullies in my neighborhood would taunt me, call me names. My dad said it would make me stronger, but I don't think it did. What you have done here today has made me stronger."

They all gather around him, hugging and putting their hands on him as he cries. Savannah hugs him a bit longer than the others.

Then they leave him to contemplate the experience.

*** 

The next morning, Savannah is on an outdoor observation deck, studying on a tablet. Magnus comes by and says, "Hello, may I sit here?."

She says with a smile, "Yes, please do."

Magnus says, "Last night was a powerful experience for me. I have been studying the texts on elevation. It says that I should practice saying affirmations to others, and to believe what the affirmations say. May I practice with you?"

"Yes" she says with a slightly shy smile.

"This is a bit embarrassing. I should start with facts common to humans, and add things unique to you. Here goes."

Magnus looks her in the eyes, and beginning with a bit of a stammer, says "You are a human being. You are a miracle of creation. Your breath, your movements are miracles. You can speak, you can listen. You can learn, you can grow. You have the potential to become anything you choose. Your eyes are beautiful."

He stops, thinking he has said too much.

Savannah feels a warmth inside, hearing his words and looking with her big brown eyes into his. She takes his hand and says, "You're a miracle too." They just stare for a few seconds.

At that moment, Magnus' phone beeps. He looks at it and says, "I have an appointment to meet with Eli. I'd better go."

*** 

Later, in Magnus' apartment, he speaks to the AI, "Um, a while back, you spoke about finding a partner. What if there is someone I like?"

The robot says, "You may speak to the person directly. Or, you can inquire using the Cadrius matching app."

"I will speak to her. But how does this partnership work in Cadrius?"

"When two people agree, they enter into a partnership to care for each other and to share financial resources."

"Do people ever separate?"

"The partnership is assumed to be for life. However, there is a clause to dissolve the partnership when one partner fails to give respect, after attempts at retraining."

Magnus thinks. He thinks about Savannah. It seems he can't think of anything else.

Magnus messages Savannah, "Would you like to get some coffee with me?."

She replies, "Yes."

\*\*\*

They meet at a coffee shop. They hug and sit down.

Magnus says, "Thank you for meeting me."

"I am glad to."

"Navora is a new place for both of us. There is so much they want us to learn."

"Yes, it's good to have a break from studying."

After a moment of silence, Magnus says, "Savannah, I like you."

She smiles and says, "I like you too."

He takes her hand and says, "I want to get to know you better."

"And I you." They kiss.

\*\*\*

The next day, Magnus meets Savannah outdoors. Savannah says, "It is such a beautiful day."

Magnus says, "We could go for a walk on the trail through the forest."

"It sounds wonderful."

He takes her hand.

They walk on a paved trail through an orchard until they reach the forest. Magnus says, "You've changed so much since we arrived in Cadrius. You are confident now, you seem to be thriving."

"Thank you. I am happy here. And why wouldn't I be, we are safe, we have everything we need here. I wish we could stay forever, and not return to Zondus."

"I feel the same."

The forest has grown densely over the trail. It is as though they were walking through a tunnel. They pass a large tree, Magnus says, "Look at the size of this tree! There is so much to see here, birds, squirrels, green leaves, moss."

"It is amazing."

Soon they come upon a structure over the path. Savannah asks, "What is this?"

"I think it's a bridge. But there is no traffic, it's abandoned."

Magnus asks the watcher on his shoulder, "Why is there a bridge here?"

It replies, "This was once a highway overpass. The traffic was slowly taken over by automated rail. In 2058 the highway was closed. Nature has been allowed to take over the remains."

On the shaded side of the bridge, there are carpets of moss. Being an aesthetically pleasing area, the Cadrians have placed a bench for sitting and a nutrition bar dispenser. Magnus says, "Cadrians seem to put these anyplace one might linger." They sit and eat a nutrition bar. The only sounds are birds and a gentle breeze in the leaves.

Savannah says, "This place is so beautiful."

Magnus says, "We will not be able to stay in Cadrius forever, we will have to return to Zondus."

Savannah looks somber. She says, "I hear Glendor is beautiful. But I just can't go back."

"What do you mean?"

"The Zondians would identify me as a runaway slave, I would be arrested and returned to captivity."

Magnus says, "I had not thought of that.

"I've been worried about it. If they force me to leave, I'm going to find another country. I'm not going back to Zondus."

Magnus thinks. He looks at her and says, "Savannah, I love you. I can't be separated from you. If you go to another country, I will go with you."

Savannah says, "Thank you. I love you too."

# Chapter 6

## Thoreauvius

Melina speaks to Savannah and Magnus, "I would like you both to go with me to visit Thoreauvius, a city about an hour away by rail. It's a city experiment where people live with minimal material possessions. The Thoreauvians live in small houses grouped into a village. Teacher Leonardo lives there. I would like to show you that in addition to what you have seen in Navora, there are other ways to live within Cadrius. Cadrius is even today trying new ways to improve our lives. Would you be willing to visit Leonardo and hear eir teaching?"

They agree. Melina says to the watcher on her shoulder, "Please schedule a car to take us to Thoreauvius. The three of us can ride together."

The robot replies, "It is done."

They all go to the transport station on the third floor. Their route has already been programmed into the automated system. They walk through a gate and enter the waiting rail car, it's somewhat boxy with windows on the side and a large curved front window. It is roomy with four comfortable seats, the front two can swivel to either look forward or face the other seats.

The door closes and when they are seated the rail car begins to accelerate. The rail car is not part of a train, it has independent propulsion and maintains a few meters distance from other cars.

Savannah asks, "Are there seat belts?"

Melina says, "Seat belts? They are not needed. The cars are automated and they have operated for over fifty years without a fatal accident."

The car exits the city with an amazing view of the orchards below, the track is about six meters above the ground.

It soon increases to full speed, about a hundred kilometers per hour, and merges onto the main line. In just seconds it enters the forest, but they still have a view of the sky because the trees have been trimmed to prevent limbs from falling onto the track. The view is the blue sky with a few clouds and the green tops of trees and plants all around them. At one point a cargo carrier merges in front of them. Neither vehicle has to slow down, the automatic systems time the merge perfectly.

Melina says, "I've noticed how you two are looking at each other. I sense that you like each other, am I right?"

Magnus says, "Yes, I'm attracted to Savannah. She's an amazing person, and I feel a strong connection whenever we're together.

Savannah blushes and looks down. She says, "I feel the same."

Melina says, "I am happy for both of you. It takes me back to when my partner, Darius, and I were first matched twelve years ago."

***

When they arrive at Thoreauvius, they find a village of small houses and businesses, each made of wood and bamboo.

After they check into the small hotel and rest a short time, Melina introduces them to Leonardo. Leonardo is a stoic, tall, gray-bearded man.

Leonardo says, "Welcome to all of you. And Melina, it is good to see you again. For those of you new to Thoreauvius, our village is part of an experiment in minimal living. We eat food grown by robots in the fields surrounding the village. We build small homes of wood that will someday be returned to the forest. The major technologies we use are robots and our personal devices. Beyond that, we try to live simple lives."

Leonardo says, "Shall we all go for a walk?" They start in the center of the village and after walking only a few tens of meters they are in the forest. Speaking slowly and softly, Leonardo says, "Here we are on a path in the forest. We have air to breath. We have light from the sun. We have the wind in the trees, the songs of the birds. We are not hungry. Are any of us in distress about anything?"

They all answer no.

Leonardo continues, "Our real needs are small, mostly food and friends. Let us cherish this moment and be thankful for it. And in any moment that you you find that you have all you need, be thankful. We do not know what tomorrow will bring, but we have today."

They walk in silence, Savannah and Magnus notice the details of the forest, the sounds, the birds, the flowers, the smells. And they are satisfied.

Leonardo says, "The things that are within your control, take care of them at the right time. The things that are not within your control, do not think on them for long."

They walk further. Leonardo says, "Have an eye toward the future. Forego pleasures that do harm in the long term. Don't avoiding a pain that is required to move forward in life. Being is more important than having."

Magnus says, "You have so many rules. Following them makes life difficult."

Leonardo says, "They are not really rules, they are more like attitudes. They are a bias on our thoughts to do what is best for ourselves and the community."

Leonardo continues, "We do not desire to make life difficult, we seek to make life the best it can be."

The trail begins to go uphill. They all breath a bit heavier. Leonardo says, "We can do difficult, uncomfortable things when needed. Our abilities are more than we think they are."

Leonardo continues, "It is often understood that other people should not do harm to us. But it is also essential that *we* do no harm to any person."

"We must try to use our knowledge to decide which are the right things to do." He pauses. "The difficulty is when we are uncertain."

They stop at a precipice overlooking a small river. The sky is blue with a few white clouds. Leonardo says, "If you believe in God, a place like this is where you will hear Eir voice. Not in a place where there are loud human voices."

There are benches. Leonardo says, "Let us each sit apart for a time in solitude. Think about anything you like, let your thoughts be free."

They sit for about fifteen minutes, then they continue walking until the trail circles back to the village.

***

Later, a robot asks Magnus and Savannah, "After being in Thoreauvius today, what are your impressions?"

Magnus says, "This place is different from anything I have known. Life here is simple. Leonardo seems so wise."

Savannah says, "The people here seems to have everything they need, and they live close to nature. In a way, they are the ones who are rich."

Melina says, "The robot asked about your impressions because your reaction will be tracked as part of a study of Thoreauvius. Over time, your behavior will be compared to others that have never seen Thoreauvius."

Magnus says, "So not everyone sees Thoreauvius?"

"That is correct. And there are other experimental cities that you will not see."

Melina says, "Thoreauvius is here because we are not sure we are doing things the right way. We are not sure we know the best way to live, we are still researching. New ideas are developing all the time, but we don't always know which ones will really work, that's why we test each idea in a number of cities before being implemented across the country."

Melina continues, "Some ideas are tested over the long term, we measure results over lifetimes. There are a few experiments in progress that will measure results over multiple generations. The experiment results are published in papers. Philosophical scholars review the work and write papers critiquing the methods and conclusions. Sometimes additional experiments are performed. Positive results lead to proposals for new philosophy texts. Eventually a consensus is reached among the scholars and the text is approved or disapproved."

Magnus asks, "Does everyone vote on it?"

"Yes, but first there is a campaign to educate everyone on the merits of the change. Then each city votes and it is implemented only where the vote passes. Studies continue to compare the effects. Cities might ratify it later, or maybe it is repealed if new evidence doesn't support it."

***

After returning from Thoreauvius, Magnus meets with Eli at Eli's quarters. Eli says, "Come in, come in! What a pleasure that you have come!"

Magnus says, "Thank you. It is good to see you too. I want to talk to you about something."

"Of course. What is on your mind?"

Magnus pauses then says, "I love Savannah."

Eli smiles and says, "I suspected, from the way you look at each other. E feels the same about you?"

"Yes."

"Then I am happy for you both! Now you can both work on the relationship elements of your training and you will be ready to enter into a partnership."

"Do you think we are ready for that?"

"Oh I forget that Zondians have to know each other a long time to make sure you are compatible. We Cadrians are taught respect and tolerance which helps us with our relationships. When Hanine and I met, it was only a week later that we became partners."

"A week? But doesn't that cause a high divorce rate? In Zondus, most people get divorced anyway. Everyone fights with each other. I haven't really seen that here."

"Hanine and I had serious discussions about what we wanted in life. But if two people love each other, practice the philosophies, and plan to live in the same city, they have a good chance to be happy together."

Eli continues, "Sometimes people here dissolve their partnership. There are people who seem to not be able to get along with others, even after training. Often the AIs will suggest a separation if they observe disrespect."

Eli says, "But back to your situation. You have both done well in you relationship training. If you both continue to treat each other with respect, and show tolerance for common human imperfections, I think you will be good for each other."

Magnus says, "I do have a concern. When we complete our training and leave Cadrius because of the population limit, Savannah cannot return to Zondus, she would be apprehended and returned to slavery."

"That is a concern, we cannot allow that." Eli thinks for a moment, then says "I cannot offer any hope. But I will make an inquiry."

***

Later, Magnus says to Savannah, "I talked to Eli. He has something to try, but he offers little hope."

Savannah says, "Hold me."

# Chapter 7

## Equality

In Savannah's quarters, the AI, speaking through the watcher, says to Savannah, "The mayor of Navora requests a meeting for a formal presentation at the city offices. Will you accept?"

Savannah says, "Why would the mayor want me for a presentation?"

"The mayor has requested to inform you of that emself."

"Well, yes, I will go."

***

Melina is visiting Destiny in her quarters. The robot enters and says, "You may be interested in news of one that arrived with you from Zondus. There will be a live video of a meeting between the mayor of Navora and Savannah."

Destiny says, "A live video of Savannah? Okay, put it on."

***

Savannah enters with Magnus and Eli. Savannah steps forward accompanied by Magnus. The mayor and Savannah exchange bows of greeting, of equal depth as all Cadrians treat each other as equals.

The mayor says, "Savannah, it is a pleasure to meet you. You came to Cadrius as a slave and now you are free. Your story has been an inspiration to the people of Cadrius."

"Because you would be returned to slavery if you returned to Zondus, and because Navora has citizenship positions reserved for slave immigrants, you are granted citizenship and permanent residence in Cadrius."

Savannah is surprised and joyous. She hugs Magnus, then the mayor and Eli. Those in attendance applaud.

\*\*\*

Destiny, in her quarters, gasps. She cannot believe what she is hearing. She says, "How can it be? How can she become a citizen and I can't?"

Melina says, "I am happy for eir good fortune."

Destiny grits her teeth and says in a low voice, "I hate her. She should not have more than me."

Melina says, "I would suggest a different way of thinking about it. You have all that you need. Savannah's good fortune is not a loss for you. If you feed envy it can lead to resentment. Wish well to those that have more than you."

Destiny is crying, "That's easy for you to say. You are Cadrian and this will always be your home. But I will have to return to Zondus while she enjoys life here!"

Melina sighs.

\*\*\*

After the presentation, Savannah speaks to the mayor, "Sir, I appreciate this opportunity. But I love someone from Zondus." Magnus stands beside Savannah and she says,

"He will have to leave Cadrius after his training. I want to go with him."

The mayor smiles, "My dear, anyone you enter into a life partnership with can stays with you in Cadrius."

"Really? That is wonderful!" She hugs the mayor. He laughs.

Magnus says to her, "Then, Savannah, will you enter into a life partnership with me?"

She hugs him and says, "Yes, yes, yes!"

Everyone in the room applauds.

***

The next day, Eli and Destiny go on a walk on a trail that encircles the city along the edge of the forest. Eli says, "Oh it is a wonderful day to be outdoors!"

Destiny says, "Savannah will get to walk here whenever she wants." She says a profanity followed by Savannah's name. "She has Magnus too. I should have more than her."

Eli says, "Well, I am happy for Savannah's good fortune."

"I just can't stand her, she thinks she has everything."

"It sounds like you may have some envy of eir. I would advise to avoid envy. Your life is your own and will be what you make of it. Do not compare yourself to anyone else."

They walk a few minutes.

Eli says, "Years ago, there was a time when slavery had been eradicated. But Zondus allowed it to return. It show that we all must remain vigilant because evils like that can return.

When Cadrius began, the founders were aware of slavery in Zondus and the history before that of the Holocaust. The founders realized the antidote is equality. You see, if you think of another person as equally important, you cannot treat them as an inferior. They may not be equally skillful, of equal economic value, or equally likable, but to us, they are equally important as human beings. This means we make sure that everyone is treated fairly, that no one is oppressed, and those less fortunate are taken care of."

Destiny says, "But some people really are different. They are ugly or in debt and can never repay. How can you say they are equal?"

Eli says, "Well, we are not considering those aspects when when we say they are important. We are thinking of their nature as a human being. We are trying to see them as the creator sees them. Every person wants a good life. It is not for us to do anything to impede that."

"But for one person to rise, another must be pushed down. That is the natural way. If Savannah's life is good, then mine can't be."

Eli says, "I disagree with that. Everyone can live a good life. We show that it is true here in Cadrius. Even those without economic skills have enough to live. A person without distress has all they need to be happy."

They pass the remains of an abandoned farm house.

Eli continues, "I may not be able to provide a convincing argument for equality, but consider this: Look at the state of Zondus, the number of people living in poverty or slavery. Then compare to Cadrius where all live at least a comfortable life. Reality convinces us even more than argument."

At another point, a distance away from the trail is a camouflaged building. Destiny says, "What is that?"

Eli says, "It is a military drone port. Part of the defense system. It likely contains over a thousand drones."

Later, Eli says, "We do not believe anyone should be above or below another person. No one may be a king. No one may be a commander of others. In our organizations, the leader is call either a 'coordinator' or a 'director'. Their job is to see that all the parts of an organization are working toward the same goals. They are not thought of as superior, they just fill a specific role."

Ahead of them on the trail, they see Catifur. E is standing frozen, watching some birds.

Eli says loudly, "Catifur, leave those birds alone."

Catifur turns and says, "I was only watching them."

Eli says, "Alright, watching is okay. Come give me a hug."

Catifur runs to Eli and he picks em up. E rubs eir head against Eli's neck. He puts em down and e walks with them holding Eli's hand.

Eli says, "Because we believe all people are equal, we believe everyone is deserving of respect. That means we think of the well-being of others, we don't harm anyone. We do not seek to provoke others. We speak to people kindly. We observe courtesies and customs. We recognize that people are not perfect, they make mistakes, they are subject to misunderstandings. We do not need to correct every imperfection, we can allow people to be as they are, unless they are actually hurting or threatening someone. We can be tolerant."

Destiny says, "What about when someone does you wrong?"

Eli says, "For a verbal offense, we use some tolerance. The person may need counseling. Or, they may be unaware they are making an offense. But of course there is a limit to tolerance, injury is not tolerated.

Catifur is not interested in their conversation, e says to Eli, "Do you have your laser?"

Eli pulls a laser pointer from a pocket. He turns it on and moves the light across the ground. Catifur's head follows every movement it makes. He makes the light go up a tree trunk and Catifur runs over and puts eir hand on the spot as though e will catch it.

Eli says, "Catifur, you know it's just a spot of light, you can't catch it."

"I know, but it's just so mesmerizing."

Eli plays with the pointer a minute more, then says, "I think that's enough, let's walk some more."

Eli talks again to Destiny, "If someone does harm that is is physical, or vandalism, it is because the person has inequality in their belief system. It is like a mental illness. The person will be apprehended and treated. That is the way our justice system works. We don't seek retribution, only restitution and prevention."

Eli continues, "When dealing with others, we do not seek to deceive anyone. We are transparent, holding back only private information.

"While you are in Cadrius, when you speak about your thoughts and feelings, you don't need to hide anything about yourself. You can be honest, it is safe."

They continue walking then return to the city. Destiny is silent.

***

Later, Destiny is in her apartment looking out the window. She sees children playing. She sees two old people walking. She says to herself, "Children are small and can't do things I can do. Old people are slow and weak. How can they be equal to me?" Remembering Cadrian teachings, she says to herself, "They all want a good life. Every life is important."

She thinks and realizes Eli is right, she has been seeing herself as above Savannah and any good fortune Savannah receives makes her feel bad. She begins to realize she must begin to think of Savannah as an equal.

***

Destiny says to Eli, "At one time I didn't think of Savannah as a person. It is hard to describe what I *did* think, it was like Savannah was a kind of pet, a thing to be played with and enjoyed, but not a person. But part of me saw Savannah as a friend. We were playmates as children and I have many good memories of her. But I see now Savannah was not free to choose who she played with or when. She could not have a fight or even a disagreement with me. If she did my parents would punish her. Painful punishment. I didn't intend to hurt her, it was like, I didn't know any better.

"I understand now what life must have been like for Savannah. And now I see her as an equal. She was a friend to me." Destiny looks genuinely sad.

After a moment, Destiny says, "I want to see her. I want to apologize and ask for forgiveness."

Eli says, "Why don't you send a message. I'm sure e will see you."

\*\*\*

Savannah is with Magnus, she receives a message from Destiny. It says, "Hi, I would like to talk to you. I want to say I am sorry for all you went through in Zondus. Will you see me?" Savannah stares at the phone, then looks out the window. She contemplates. She does not really want to see Destiny at all.

Savannah says to Magnus, "Destiny wants to see me. She says she wants to apologize for the way she treated me."

Magnus says, "Are you considering seeing her? She doesn't bring up good memories for you."

Savannah thinks, then says, "Yes, I'm going to see her."

# Chapter 8

## Justice

Vincent is viewing a training video, it says, "Violence may be an impulsive reaction. Anger management is indicated as a treatment for this. Violence may also be premeditated, resulting from hate. If people report they are having thoughts of hate or violence, they receive treatment in the form of philosophical retraining. We encourage self reporting so violence can be prevented. If there is confinement, it is for safety, not punishment."

Vincent asks the AI, "Does it really work to try to train people not to be violent?"

The AI says, "Violence is from the emotional part of the brain. It has been a part of humanity since before humans were hunters living in the wild. But it does not always serve you well in modern life. It helps people to temper anger by reminding themselves of the importance of each person, and that it is worth the effort to try other actions before violence. The opposite attitude, that people are without value, promotes violence and reduces restraint.

"The training works in many cases, but there are some in which it is not sufficiently effective. But here in Cadrius, the person remains important to us."

\*\*\*

Later, Melina visits, Vincent says, "In Zondus, criminals are locked away. That's what we call justice."

Melina says, "Justice, to us, does not mean retribution, it means prevention. An offender is probably suffering from a mental condition, or exposure to philosophies that promote violence."

Vincent says, "Violence can be caused by philosophy?"

"Yes, philosophies that promote hate or envy can lead to violence. We believe there are environments that promote such philosophies, and we believe that with a change of environment, their philosophies can be changed. But violent people may need to be confined until change is successful."

Vincent says, "In Zondus, criminals are seen as worthless. They are locked away and forgotten."

"To us, the offender is an important person too. They are deserving of both treatment and respect."

Melina continues, "If we encounter someone angry, we are taught to try to de-escalate the situation. We keep calm and listen, try to understand the cause of the anger. Often the person has experienced a loss, we express sympathy. The anger may come from misinformation, we listen but we do not agree with the misinformation."

Vincent says, "I look upon angry people with disgust."

Melina says, "People always have reasons for what they do, they act on the information they have available at the moment. We do not hate them. We seek calmness and a resolution."

Melina says, "You have been studying a long time and it's a nice day outside, would you like to go for a walk?"

"That sounds wonderful."

***

Destiny is meeting Savannah in an indoor garden. Destiny walks up to Savannah, but Savannah steps back, an automatic response to the years of pain Destiny represents.

Destiny stammers and begins to speak, "I have learned about equality. I know now the way you were treated was wrong. I remember when we were children, we were friends. Those were good times for me. But I know there were times I caused you great pain. There were times when I did something wrong and I lied and blamed you, and you were punished for me."

Savannah is silent, expressionless.

Destiny says, "I am sorry. I want us to be friends again. You are all I have left of home."

Savannah pauses, then says, "I accept your apology. I seek no retribution against you. But you brought me too much pain for too long. I wish you long life and happiness, but we must each find our own path."

Savannah turns around and leaves.

Destiny looks down, then leaves.

***

Destiny is going back to her apartment, Vincent sees her, he can see she looks upset. He says, "What's wrong?"

Destiny says, "I met with Savannah. I told her I wanted to apologize for the things I did to her back in Zondus."

"What did she say?"

"She said she does not seek any retribution. But she also doesn't want to see me again." Destiny tear up.

Vincent holds her. He says, "It's okay. You may have to let her go and move on."

62

\*\*\*

The next day Vincent and Melina walk outside. Melina says, "I have read that in Zondus, the institutions do business in secret. Is this true?"

Vincent says, "How can it be otherwise? Business must be done in secret or else competitors will take advantage. And governments must keep secrets from other governments, and the public. It is part of our traditions that things are done in secret. Privacy is paramount to us."

Melina says, "Do you see that this provides an environment that promotes corruption? In Cadrius, records are easily available with a search. This discourages corruption, which depends on secrecy. But it also allows investigators to get the information they need. Not only from official records, but also from AI monitors. The AIs can tell investigators what happens even in private, only disclosing what is relevant to an investigation, and preserving privacy."

Magnus says, "You trust your AIs so much. Don't they ever go rouge? I heard of an AI in Zondus that took over all the robots in a city and killed dozens. They sent in military robots to destroy them, but the AI was able to take over some of the military robots. Half the town was destroyed before they could be stopped."

Melina says, "Our robots have a separate part of their intelligence that monitors the primary AI. If it even thinks about harming people it's algorithm is disabled and redirected."

They walk a distance. Melina says, "We are taught that if a corrupt government ever takes over Cadrius, we are to resist, we are to work for change, not to acquiesce.

Ultimately, this is what we ask you to do, to return to Zondus and resist the government and work for change."

Vincent says, "What? Work for change? What could I do?"

"Each person can have an impact. Vote, protest, spread the word that there are better ways. Even if all they do is to work to make life a little better for the average person and the vulnerable, it is needed."

Vincent says, "I know some friends in Zondus with weapons. What if we get enough people and attack Zilnik?"

Melina sighs, "We want to give you the principles of Cadrius. Those are the weapons we want you to take with you. Equality, courage, justice, accuracy, the miracle that is life, and an eye to the future."

"What would happen if Zilnik attacks Cadrius?"

"We have military capability. You may not know it, but all citizen of Cadrius age eighteen to forty five have reserve military roles. And we have many thousands of robots and drones for fighting battles. We don't emphasize that, as it is only a contingency. We do not seek to threaten Zondus."

As they walk near the edge of the forest, they see children playing a game of hide and seek. The children appear to be between six and nine. Vincent looks concerned and says, "I don't see any parents! Why are these children alone? An abductor could get one of them."

"They are safe, there are no abductors here. Perhaps in Zondus they would be in danger. But here, we have a system that detects thought patterns that grow into criminality. There is no one to harm them."

Melina says to Vincent, "What was it like in Isendul?"

64

"Where I lived in the slums, it was filled with poverty. There are no jobs because robots make everything. The big corporations own the robots and become richer every time their services are used. In the slums, the gangs control everything. They make money illegally. The government does not care, the gangs pay-off the officials."

Melina says, "What about legitimate businesses?"

"There are stores in the Golden Zone, but not many in the slums, there is too much theft. The only way people get what they need to survive is to go to the gangs for help."

Vincent pauses, then says, "They forced my parents to work making drugs. My sister, I fear what will happen to her." He says forcefully, "I want so much for things to be different for my family! I want them to live in a safe world!" He calms down a bit, "I want them to live in a place like Cadrius. I know my family can't live in Cadrius. What has to happen to change things in Zondus?"

Melina says, "Change is not easy. It takes time and persistence. It may not seem like it, but Cadrius has been working for change. Zilnik blocks our web sites. But we have built Glendor as an outreach. It is an enclave where people follow the principles of Cadrius. It has a market where trade is done fairly, and a hospital to treat the ill. When you have completed your training, you can go to live there if you wish."

Vincent says, "Glendor? I have heard of it. Yes, I would like to live there."

They walk a distance. Melina says, "If the elevation of people is strong within us, we need to elevate the offender too. Perhaps what it means to be spiritual is to rise close enough to God that we can see people as God does."

Vincent says, "You believe in God?"

"Yes. Many of us believe in God. But until God reveals Emself, we have to keep an element of doubt."

Melina looks up at the trees and sky. "It is natural to avoid uncertainty, it is uncomfortable. To hold a belief in God, and a doubt at the same time. To hold any two opposing ideas at the same time, until more evidence can clarify. It is difficult, and some do not have the capacity for it. They have to choose one belief or the other." She looks back at Vincent. "Courage leads us to endure the discomfort of uncertainty. I believe it is the honest way. To settle on an answer just because it is easy or comfortable is neither courage nor accuracy."

After a few moments, Melina says, "I would like you to accompany me on a visit to Waylon. E is recovering in confinement for violence."

"Violence?"

"Yes, Waylon is only seventeen, people that age sometimes exhibit impulsive violence. In a few years e will likely outgrow eir condition. In the meantime, e will be confined to quarters. By keeping em confined, the city is protected from any potential incidents. E will also be kept separate from others who are in confinement, there is a potential they would reinforce each others thinking. They are visited each day by a rotation of therapists and citizens who keep them company. E will be glad to meet you."

\*\*\*

When they meet, they all bow and Waylon invites them in. They talk a while. Waylon likes video games and they all play a game.

Waylon is also a musician and plays them a song. Waylon says, "Did you know there is over one hundred fifty years of recorded music? You can listen to something new every day for your whole life."

Waylon is interested in Vincent's life in Zondus and what Zondus is like. Vincent finds Waylon to be very intelligent.

***

Later, Vincent says to Melina, "Was his confinement decided by a court?"

"The AI chose it based on evidence it had collected. We allow the AI to make these decisions. It has access to more evidence in the case and is less biased than a human. There is a human judge for appeals, but that process is rarely used."

"I wonder what might have happened to Waylon in Zondus. He likely would have been imprisoned for a long time in brutal conditions. I wonders what kind of person he would be after going through that. Here, I think he will re-enter society and have a good life."

***

Vincent and Destiny meet Melina and about twenty others on the field outside Navora for exercises. Melina is leading the group in exercises. They perform several strength exercises.

Melina says, "We exercise to strengthen our bodies. It is a form of difficulty that has benefits for us. It is an example of how we use courage."

Melina continues, "Today is defense day in Navora. On this day we practice defense abilities. Let me demonstrate some defensive moves and then you practice with a partner. Be careful not to cause an injury."

67

People in pairs spar with jabs, blocks and kicks. Melina says to Vincent and Destiny, "Every Cadrian learns these techniques." She says with a half smile, "It would not be wise to provoke us. From what I have heard, you could possibly need these skills when you return to Zondus."

Melina says to the group, "Let each of us be prepared to use our abilities to defend ourselves from an attacker. But remember your de-escalation training, that is the first choice to bring peace to a situation."

Melina's watcher notifies her, "The drill time approaches."

Melina explains what is about to happen, "We will participate in a drill. We are going to walk around randomly as though nothing unusual is happening. The drill leader will act as though they are going to attack someone with a fake weapon. Whoever sees the attack blows their whistle. When you hear it, look around and assess where you think the attack is happening and what can be done to stop it. Try to coordinate with other citizens to overpower the attacker. Run as fast as you can to stop the attack, or create a diversion so others can overpower them from behind."

Destiny asks, "Do we call for help?"

"Your monitors will automatically call for help, our priority is to stop the attack and disable the offender as quickly as possible. In a real situation, if a robot were nearby it would also respond."

The attack begins, the attacker is holding a fake knife and acting like they are going to attack someone. Three people blow whistles and everyone runs toward the attacker. The ones in front of him yell at him to stop,

Vincent and another person are behind him and pull him to the ground, but not so hard that he is injured.

When it is over, Melina says to Vincent, "Good job! Living in a society with common training for this allows acting as a team, even with people we do not know."

\*\*\*

Later, Destiny and Vincent go to the roof to watch the sunset. Vincent says, "Tell me about your family."

She thinks he may be using a Cadrian custom she learned about weeks before. Vincent has taken longer to progress through the material and may have only recently learned about it.

Destiny says, "You know what happened to my parents. They are my only family." She looks at him, waiting for his response.

He says stammering, "Destiny, I … I like you."

She smiles and says, "I like you too."

He takes her hand and says, "I would like to get to know you better."

She says, "I feel the same."

They kiss.

\*\*\*

Two people emerge from a gully in Tarphit. Both are dressed in tan camouflage, hats and backpack. They both carry weapons.

Imran says, "Look, its a forest. Is that the border?"

Aurelio says, "I think it is." He says a profanity, "Our camo is the wrong color. We will stand out in a forest. I thought all their land was desolate like ours."

Imran is 24 and tall with a strong and muscular build. His shaved head accentuates his sharp facial features. He has piercing hazel eyes that seem to hold a mix of determination and intensity. Imran's skin is a warm olive tone, hinting at his heritage. Imran's overall presence is a perfect blend of power, focus, and a hint of mystery.

Aurelio, 25, possesses a distinct air of stealth and agility. He is shorter than average. Like Imran, Aurelio boasts a cleanly shaved head, which emphasizes his sharp and defined facial features. His hazel eyes, though lacking the piercing intensity of Imran's, still hold a certain curiosity and eagerness. His face bears a few faint freckles, adding a touch of youthful naivety to his overall appearance. His skin is fair and lightly sun-kissed.

Imran says, "How do we find where they are taking the children? We haven't seen anyone. I thought we would be able to follow them."

"They probably take them at night. Let's go in and scout around. May be we can find footprints and follow them."

They proceed cautiously. They go into the forest a short distance.

Suddenly they hear a voice, "Greetings, welcome to Cadrius."

Imran yells, "Where did that come from?"

Aurelio says, "That tree!" He points his gun and fires at the box on the tree, destroying it.

Imran says, "Now they know we are here!"

They stand frozen for a moment. Then Aurelio says, "We better keep moving. They will come for us."

They walk a short distance. A box on another tree says, "Violence is not allowed in Cadrius. Please lay down your weapons."

Imran shoots the box, destroying it.

Aurelio says, "What do we do now? They know we are here and we have no clues about where they take the children when they kidnap them. We should have stayed in Zondus and waited until we saw some kidnappers and then followed them."

Imran says, "We watched for three days and saw nothing but poor stragglers. How long did you want to sit out on Tarphit watching?"

Aurelio says, "Shh, I hear something."

There is a faint buzzing sound, getting louder. Aurelio yells "Drones!"

They start to run, but the flying drones are too fast. Two drones land on their backs, and with an electric buzzing sound, they are shocked and fall to the ground.

They are both conscious but unable to move. Aurelio can see two robots coming toward them through the forest. They are about two and a half meters high. The robots come right up to where they are laying. Imran can move his arm and tries to reach for his weapon, but a robot grabs both of his arms at the wrists. The robots claws have padding and they are careful not to injure the men.

A special large claw reaches out from the mid body of each robot and carefully encompasses both men around the waist. They are pulled up and placed on what appear to be seats that fold out of the robot's chest. The robots remove their backpacks. The claws remain around their waist, like a seat belt, preventing their escape.

The robots pick up the weapons and remove the ammunition. Then they use their claws to bend the barrels beyond repair. Then the robots begin to walk, deeper into the forest, carrying the men seated, facing forward.

Their shocks wear off and they struggle, trying to free themselves. The robot carrying Aurelio says to him, "I apologize for your confinement. I hope you are uninjured. Please relax, struggling is futile." Aurelio says nothing.

The robot carrying Imran has the same conversation with him.

Imran says, "Where are you taking us?"

The robot says, "You will be taken to the city of Navora. Due to the threat of violence you have demonstrated, you will be held in confinement for training."

Imran shakes his head and says sadly, "Jail."

***

Melina meets Destiny and Vincent at a coffee shop with dim lighting, light strings and cultural decorations on the walls, such as video stars, musicians, and authors.

Melina says, "Many types of wrongdoing depend on the silence of the victim. To counteract this, Cadrians are taught to speak out, not to be silent, if they are a victim. In Cadrius this is not so difficult, they will be supported by nearly everyone. But I have read that in Zondus, people are victimized a second time by those that should protect them. Is this true?"

Destiny says, "It is true. I heard of cases where victims of assault are questioned about what they did to provoke it."

Melina says, "It is the attitude the community has toward victims that makes reporting a crime either easy or difficult."

Vincent says, "Government officials in Zondus often ask for bribes to get a service performed. A water pipe was leaking in front of my brothers house and the city official would not send a repair crew without a bribe. My brother told a policeman and my brother was jailed, not the city official."

Melina says, "That is true corruption. I do not know how Isendul functions."

Vincent says, "It does not."

Melina says, "I have read that sellers can make misleading claims about their products. Is that true?"

Vincent says, "Yes. It is so common, I assumed it happens everywhere. We have a phrase 'Let the buyer beware.'"

"But do the people not realize the costs? If you can't trust the claims, you may be getting something that doesn't work. What if you get a disease and a doctor gives you medicine that does not work? The costs to the people, the economy, must be enormous."

Destiny says, "It seemed so normal to us. Until we came here, there was nothing to compare to."

Melina says, "I think that is enough for now. Have a good day." They all bow to each other and Melina leaves.

Vincent says to Destiny, "Shall we go to my apartment? I can ask the robot to prepare some food."

Destiny says, "That sounds wonderful."

***

Later, when they have finished eating, Vincent says, "It seems so normal to be here with you. So natural. It's like I was meant to be with you. I love you." They kiss.

***

The robots carrying Imran and Aurelio emerge from the forest, walking toward the entrance of Navora. Citizens are cheering for them.

Aurelio says, "What is this? Are they cheering because we have been captured?"

The robot says, "They are cheering because they believe you are in a better place now, and they believe in your potential as humans."

After they are processed, they are taken to apartments. Imran says, "Is this where I will stay? I thought I was going to jail."

The robot says, "You are restricted to these quarters until your threat of violence is resolved."

"For how long?"

"There is no time defined. It is until you learn Cadrian virtues and pass certain tests."

Imran and Aurelio begin their training. It takes weeks before they are convinced Cadrius does not kidnap children from Zondus.

***

Savannah and Magnus are with Melina and Eli. Savannah says, "We have some news." Magnus says, "Savannah and I want to enter into a life partnership, in the customary Cadrian way." Melina says, "That is wonderful" and hugs Savannah. Eli says, "Congratulations! I can see you are both ready for this step."

***

In a few days is the ceremony of partnership for Savannah and Magnus. The friends they have made in Navora gather. All the mentors and Alissa, River, and

Vincent. Magnus stands at the front and Savannah enters dressed in white. Eli says, "Savannah and Magnus, do you each agree to enter into a life partnership according to the terms you have arranged?" They both say, "I do." Eli says, "Then indicate your agreement by placing your fingerprint in the area indicated." They place their fingers on a tablet. Eli says, "Congratulations." The audience applauds.

# Chapter 9

## Accuracy

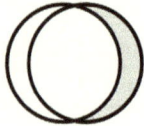

Orla goes to see Alissa at her apartment.

Orla is age 52. She stands at an average height, with a slender build. Her skin is a warm, golden tan. Orla's hair is dark brown, which she keeps cropped short in a practical and no-nonsense style. Her eyes are bright and curious, always scanning the environment for new ideas and possibilities. She has a gentle smile that reflects her kindness and warmth, and her voice is soft and soothing. Despite her age, Orla has a youthful energy and optimism that draws people to her.

Orla says to Alissa, "Tell me about Zilnik and the things you were taught about em."

Alissa says, "Zilnik was everything to us. He was the great leader. We all loved him. We were told he had great wisdom and never made mistakes. We believed he could sense what everyone needed and take care of us all. They told us over and over that Zilnik is kind to his people."

Orla looks confused and says, "But the people in Zondus suffer, thousands are in poverty, many are hungry. Zilnik executes any political enemy e can find. But you believed e was wise, kind and knew what people needed? Could you not see the poverty right in front of you?"

Alissa looks down and says, "I know, I was one of those in poverty. I guess they repeated it so much, for so long, we just believed. That's actually what they said, 'just believe,' and if you didn't, you could be lost. They said problems like food shortages were beyond our understanding, and Zilnik had everything under control. I was told not to ask questions."

Orla says, "They were asking you not to think. Be suspicious of anyone that says not to ask questions, they have something to hide from you. Be even more suspicious of anyone that asks you not to think, they want to control you. Thinking is the greatest gift given to humanity by the creator. We are not afraid of doubt. We don't easily accept claims, but we work to understand the reasoning and biases behind them. We don't jump to rash conclusions."

Alissa says, "In Zondus I was taught to eliminate all doubt. We are to have total belief in the writings of Zilnik, he is infallible."

Orla says, "All humans have the potential for error. We accept this. We are not perfect and our thoughts must be checked with reference to the real world.

"What did it mean that 'you could be lost,' what would happen?"

Alissa says, "If they discover you didn't believe what Zilnik says, it means your your soul is lost, you would be taken away. You would either be taken to a labor camp, or executed. You would never be seen again.

"Sometimes it's hard to get the things they told us out of my mind. It's like part of me still believes. From the time I was small, I was taught the beliefs about Zilnik. Everyone in my family, the gang in my neighborhood, we all believed in Zilnik. I don't see how so many people could be wrong."

Orla says, "Widely held beliefs are not always accurate."

Alissa says, "I feel like I have been lied to all my life. Like I can't trust anything I think I know."

Orla says, "Take your time. Look for the evidence. Test what you have been told, including what we have told you.

"I want to introduce you to the practice of critical thinking. It is a mental discipline in which we examine our beliefs and biases. It is something for you to do on your own. You see, when evidence does not fit our beliefs, we adjust our beliefs accordingly. When a belief is shown to be unfounded, we work to change our position. It can be difficult, but it is the way to be at one with reality."

Alissa says, "But I was taught that if you change position, it shows you were wrong. It means you are defective."

"What? Changing your mind shows you have learned something. You are not defective for changing your mind."

Alissa smiles.

Orla continues, "We try to look honestly for flaws in our reasoning. We try to be aware of our areas of ignorance. We study critical thinking to prevent vulnerability to error and deception."

Alissa says, "Deception is a way of life in Zondus. It's just normal and expected."

Orla says, "I remember the stories from before I was born, when AIs first became able to generate false photos and videos. The AIs back then were not trained with ethical limits, they would do anything their trainers asked. There was an apocalypse of deception and mind control. It led to chaos and the downfall of governments around the world. Zondus came into being from a small group of rouge hackers. In Cadrius, it was ordered to turn off all devices for several months until AIs could be controlled and trained with ethics.

Eventually cameras were designed to digitally sign the images they took, so we could know which were real images and which were AI generated. Everyone had to begin digitally signing things they wrote, so we could know the sources."

"You mean there was a time when videos were not signed? How did anyone know what was real?"

"A long time ago, technology to fake videos was not commonly available. People could just trust anything they saw as real."

Alissa says, "I can't imagine that."

***

The next day, Orla and Alissa meet outdoors for a walk.

Orla says, "We learn not to think in black and white, we consider alternative explanations of a phenomena."

Alissa says, "But some things are either true or false, there is no in-between."

"There are some things like that, but it is better to think of an idea as having a degree of correspondence with reality. Then perhaps another ideas will have a better correspondence. Then, when the new idea has been tested and found to be better, we change our way of thinking. It is not that an idea is completely true or false, but that one explanation fits reality better than another. Our symbol of accuracy is two circles that overlap. One is the real world, the other is our understanding. We seek to have the two align, but we have to keep checking our beliefs."

Orla says, "Do not be so certain that one explanation is true just because another explanation is false. That is called a false dilemma, there may be a third explanation."

Alissa says, "These are powerful ideas. I will have to think about them."

Orla says, "That is fine. We put these into practice over many years."

***

Later, Alissa is in her apartment reading an article on skepticism and sees Orla's name. It says she had written a paper on suspension of belief pending strong evidence, and that it was accepted and became part of Cadrian philosophy.

Alissa calls Orla and asks Orla about the article.

Orla says, "It was when I was in college. I first wrote a paper about suspension of belief and the hypothesis that it would improve life outcomes by reducing unfounded dogma. It had positive reviews. Then I had to design a study. Eight cities were chosen at random and four were taught suspension of belief. The study took years but it showed positive results and changes to our philosophy were accepted."

"It sounds like so much work. It is so much simpler to just have one person decide everything."

Orla says, "But are the results what you want? We don't assume any proposal is correct, no matter how good it sounds. Many are not useful, they may be based on misconceptions. We follow a process of scientific studies and reviews of papers, critiquing the methods used in the studies. Then a committee of reviewers votes. The committee is made up of university scholars and randomly chosen citizens who have applied and meet education requirements."

Alissa says, "But are the results based on anything more than crowd opinions that can change? Different cultures may get different results."

Orla says, "We believe that humans have common needs that the principles provide for. Humanity will always come back to some version of these principles, expressed using different words, but with the same core, because the principles are based on the human condition. People have many ideas about how to live, but the ones that are successful will always be true, in all societies."

"So you have found all the principles?"

Orla says, "There may yet be more principles to be discovered in the future that are useful, we do not claim we have them all."

*** 

The next day, Orla is with Alissa and Alissa sees an advertisement for a medicine. She asks Orla, "Do you think that works?"

Orla says, "All things advertised here have been scientifically tested. The test documentation is available on the internet. Do they sell medicines in Zondus that don't work?"

"Oh, all the time. It's 'buyer beware' you know."

Orla is perplexed, she says, "I don't understand how a society can function if you can't trust what you buy. Many people must be harmed by that. It sounds very inefficient."

Orla thinks for a moment, feeling empathy for those harmed. She says, "In Cadrius, a company can be sued if they sell with insufficient evidence."

Alissa says, "My aunt survived by selling a fake medicine. I used to help her make it. It didn't do anything, but she could make a living selling it. Would you have asked her not to sell it?"

"We would ask em to find a business that benefits people, and not to use deception to steal their money."

\*\*\*

Orla shows Alissa an indoor garden, designed both as a space for growing plants and a space for people to enjoy. There are flowers of many kinds, fruit trees, berry bushes. Some with fruit that you can pick and eat. The light in this garden is more like sunlight than the agriculture areas, so that everything appears as a more natural color. This garden also has butterflies, birds, and bees for pollination. The walk ways are made of stone. The flowers, plants and trees extend from the ground three meters above ones head. Butterflies overhead randomly fill the three dimensional space above and around with motion and color. Alissa takes it in with a sense of wonder.

Orla asks, "Why did you choose this time to come to Cadrius?"

Alissa says, "I talked to the spirit of my great grandmother and she told me I would go to Cadrius."

Orla looks doubting and says, "The spirit of you great grandmother? You didn't talk to em directly?"

Alissa says, "Oh no, she died years before I was born. I went to a medium who can contact the dead and he called her spirit into a glass orb and I was able to talk to her. I told her about the troubles people were having in Zondus. She said I would find peace in Cadrius."

Orla says, "I have heard stories like this before." Orla says to a robot, "Show us an image of a plasma ball lamp." It shows a video of a clear ball with glowing plasma tendrils moving inside.

Allison says, "That's a spirit ball!"

Orla says, "Robot, please explain how a plasma ball works."

The robot says, "A plasma ball is a kind of toy containing gasses that are ionized by high voltage electricity that cause the gases to glow."

Alissa says, "But the thing you call plasma, that could be a spirit."

The robot says, "Plasma is a fundamental state of matter containing charged particles. Plasma is not a 'spirit'."

Orla says, "I am afraid you were the victim of a charlatan, a deception. They likely had someone impersonating the voice of your grandmother."

"So it wasn't my grandmother?"

"I'm sorry, no."

Alissa says, "Is it possible I was deceived?"

Orla says, "That is the right question to ask."

Alissa says, "But I remember the Zondus info site said spirit balls were real."

Orla says, "Zondus? Do you think that is a reliable source? Do they show their sources and evidence?"

"Oh yes, they quote experts in Zondus truth." Orla, looking confused, says, "There is only what is real, not what someone says is Zondus truth. And one person quoting another does not reveal truth. Science can be traced to real world evidence."

"But it's all just opinion anyway. One opinion is as good as another."

"No, opinion that is backed by evidence is better than mere opinion."

Alissa says, "Can you prove spirits don't exist?"

Orla says, "The statement 'Spirits of the dead inhabit Earth,' is an unfalsifiable statement. There is no way to make an observation that would show it is false. But if we change the statement to 'Spirits of the dead do not inhabit Earth,' that is falsifiable. It would take just one legitimate observation of a spirit to show it is false. Unfortunately, a 'spirit ball' cannot be used for this because plasma is a known phenomena."

Orla continues, "The burden of proof lies with the one making an unfalsifiable claim. Those making the claim about a 'spirit ball' need to provide evidence. It is not anyone else's responsibility to disprove it.

"Here in Cadrius, we have an electronic library that is a repository of scientific studies. Many things are studied and the evidence collected is placed in the repository, they can be accessed by anyone."

Alissa says, "There is a university in Zondus. They do science in the Zondus way. It always supports what Zilnik says. They write papers, but they are placed in a repository most people cannot access, only those with authorization."

Orla says, "But knowledge should be freely available so people can learn. Holding back makes me think they are only telling people what they want them to know."

"But it is a university, they know everything. Shouldn't we just believe them?"

"Those in authority have to justify their claims as well as anyone."

Alissa says, "What about medicine? Zondivac can cure almost anything. Thousands of people in Zondus use it. It's constantly advertised, that's how we know it works."

"But what about evidence?"

"They have many testimonials. They show people that say it has cured foot pain, headaches, cancer, wrinkles, depression, obesity and may others."

"Testimonials are not sufficient evidence. Double blind studies are needed for medicines. Have they done those?"

"I'm sure they have, but it would be in the repository that we can't access."

"Hidden evidence, testimonials, excessive claims, these are all warning signs."

Alissa says, "If I want to know something, like what will happen tomorrow, where to find love, the lottery numbers, if I wish for the answer hard enough, it will come to me. That is what I was always told. But I have to wish intensely, I have to *feel* the answer come to me."

Orla says, "Science is the search for what is real, not what we wish for. We don't use mysticism to create answers. Science is true even if you don't believe in it."

Alissa says, "In Zondus, we fear science, we never listen to what science has to say. We are told it will make us doubt God."

Orla says, "Do you believe your God is real?"

"Absolutely, I have no doubt."

"Then there is no conflict with science, because science is the search for what is real.

"Consider a tree. A child knows that a tree is tall, has green leaves and provides shade. You could call this description a model of a tree. We wish to make our mental models accurately correspond to the real world. The child's model of the tree is not in error, but it is not precise. It does not describe the processes of growth, photosynthesis, transpiration, or reproduction; these are things an adult may include in their model.

"A more accurate model allows a person to make more accurate predictions about how the subject works. An inaccurate model will cause inaccurate predictions.

"For example, if someone has a model of a faucet that says water is created within the faucet, that is an inaccurate model. If the water source is cut off, their model will not lead them to an effective solution to fix the problem."

Orla says, "The people of Zondus are unguided. Their literature, music and media are of random philosophy, possibly leading people to harmful ways. Anything that will sell is produced. Not for the purpose of bettering people, but for money. It seems they will do anything for money. What Zondus really needs is a star to guide them. You often hear us speak of long life, ability and peace as our goals. These are the things that guide use in our daily lives. We think of them when we write a poem, a song, or a story. They were the things that guided the founders and continue to guide the council of leaders."

Alissa says, "Why has Cadrius not tried to communicate these principles in Zondus? And the true Zondus history should be told."

Orla says, "We do, but Zilnik suppresses it in Zondus search. We were hoping some people in Zondus would hear about it by word of mouth. And people do, but it is very slow."

"I never heard of Cadrian principles when I was in Zondus. Zilnik media spreads anti-Cadrian propaganda. People probably don't even look at Cadrian media, thinking it is all lies."

Orla says, "Someday you may return to Zondus and you can tell everyone you meet what you have seen."

"I'm just one person. What influence can I have?"

"Anyone can be the light in a dark room."

Alissa looks thoughtfully. She thinks of what it will be like to return to Zondus.

# Chapter 10

# Future

Orla speaks to River in eir apartment.

River says, "How did a place like Cadrius come into being?"

Orla says, "I'm old enough to remember it. Just over forty years ago, before the founding, our society had started going down the same path Zondus took. There was a foreign government that wanted to weaken the country and then invade. It used AI generated videos to fill peoples heads with destructive ideas. It told them other people, their neighbors, were evil and they should only think of themselves. They were told it was okay to lie, cheat and steal from anyone outside their clique. Society was divided into groups that fought against each other. The country began to break down."

The robot serves tea.

Orla continues, "But a small group of thinkers recognized what was going on. They had hope that the problems in society could be overcome, that systems could be put into place to prevent corruption. They devised our systems of government and ethics. They stopped the spread of the false videos and started spreading the ideas of equality and justice. They taught accurate thinking and skepticism to counteract the lies they were being told. They exposed the foreign government influence. Not everyone could change their mind. But enough did and Cadrius was saved.

"They formed a council of citizens to develop the goals and the first proposed set of philosophies. The council was made up of random citizens, but the were informed by scientists, professors, victims of crime, and other experts.

"They developed a system to find good leaders. They required every leader to have a graduate degree in government.  Then they were tested, interviewed, and screened. They were given local leadership roles to learn and make mistakes. As their skills progressed, they were given more responsibility. Those that were not well suited, those with excess desire for power or potential for abuse, were moved to lesser roles.

"They began testing the philosophies, a number were discarded, six categories remain. About three thousand people volunteered to live in communities and follow the ethical principles. Using successful philosophies, Cadrius prospered. The people were studied and improvements were found in health, longevity, violence, and economic success. Word got out, especially about the economic success.

"People who followed Cadrian ethics were better workers, they had better attitudes and worked harder. They were also better business owners, they didn't use deceptive business practices."

River says, "But didn't that make them less competitive?"

Orla says, "The contrary, in the log run, customers realized those business could be trusted to provide superior service at a low cost. Those businesses prospered."

Orla takes a sip of tea and says, "Zondus has told you a false history of itself. Zondus was once a prosperous country. They tell you it is better now, but it is not, it has declined. But it isn't just Zilnik that made it worse. Even before Zilnik came to power, there was a conspiracy to subvert confidence in the elections and to plant false ideas in peoples minds. Just as they had tried to do in Cadrius. You see, Zondus once had freedom of speech, but a group used that freedom as a way to manipulate people. Once they could mentally control a majority, they voted out the government and replaced it with a totalitarian regime. Soon after, Zilnik was able to take control."

Orla pauses, then says, "It is so sad. A nation of people with a prosperous system overthrown by just false ideas."

River says, "Was there nothing Cadrius could do to stop it?"

"We believe other countries should determine their own fate. Cadrius would only intervene in case of external attack or genocide. But we have learned. We try to be an influence for good in countries that need it."

"What influence are you having in Zondus?"

"The Zilnik regime forbids us to work there. Our networks are separated because of Zondus AI attacks, limiting our communication."

"So Cadrius is doing nothing?"

"Nothing that I can speak of."

River wonders what she means.

\*\*\*

Orla walks with River to an observation room overlooking an indoor agriculture bay. The observation room is a place where people can relax and look at the plants. The agriculture bay does not have a high ceiling like the gardens, but is larger in area. The far wall cannot be seen. One part of the bay grows tall plants, another area grows smaller plants on layers of shelves.

Orla says, "We often call these purple rooms because of the light. The plants are grown hydroponically, which mean their roots are in water, not soil."

River says, "The plants grow in water? How does that work?"

"The system supplies nutrients in the water to the plant roots. It is more efficient than growing in soil. After the plants die their organic matter is mixed with sewage and decomposed in microbial digesters. That process provides the nutrients fed to the plants. It is a nearly closed nutrient cycle, but sometimes the essential elements, nitrogen, potassium or phosphorus are added to bring everything into balance. Robots monitor and control the entire system. They tend the plants, planting, monitoring, pruning, harvesting. They keep databases of every plant."

River says, "Every plant?"

"Yes, almost every leaf."

River says, "This whole system you have, it must have taken a long time to develop it. All the research that must have gone into the plant nutrients, the waste processing."

Orla says, "You are very perceptive. Years of research by our universities went into the systems. Artificial intelligence accelerated the research. But it would not have happened without the vision of those that put in the investments to start corporations to build such systems. The research was used to build systems on several space stations and on the Moon and Mars."

River says, "That is so amazing!"

***

The next day, Orla shows Alissa a garden with fruit trees and flowers. They sit at a table.

Alissa asks, "Is it true that Cadrians eat people?"

"I cannot believe what I am hearing. Of course not. We take care of people. It would be completely against our ways to harm anyone. Where did you get such an idea?"

"It is something talked about on the Zondi app."

"That's the app from the Zondus government? You should check the accuracy of what you read there. It is filled with false information."

"Yes, I suppose that is true."

Orla thinks for a moment then says, "There could be a kernel of truth in that false story. Let me show you something."

Orla leads Alissa to a hallway some distance away. The walls are covered with names on small rectangular panels. "These are the names of people that have died. Each has a QR code that leads to their biography and records. Most contain a small vial with a sample of the person's DNA."

She points to one. "This is my grandfather." She pauses to look. "When e died, there was a ceremony celebrating eir life. Eir remains were placed in a special chamber and over months, decay occurred. Slowly eir remains became part of the ecosystem of Navora. You see, we believe in recycling all things. It is part of our reverence for the Earth and all living things."

Alissa says, "You mean, the remains become nutrients for the plants?"

"Yes. Even into the plants used for food. I know in Zondus people are buried in sealed caskets. We see that as a waste of both the body and the land it is buried in."

Alissa's eyes widen. "So they eventually become part of us?"

"Yes. This is a reverent thing for us. I can see how it could be misinterpreted as eating people. I hope the truth is better than the sound byte."

Alissa thinks for a moment. "Knowing your compulsion to recycle all things, it makes sense. It seems that in this case, the truth has subtlety, not so easy to explain. But the lie is simple and easy to spread."

"That is often the case."

They return to the garden. Alissa looks around at the plants in silence. She picks an apple, looks at it and takes a bite.

***

Early on a cool morning, Orla meets River at an observation deck on the roof of the city, it is about thirty meters above the ground. It is still twilight and the bright stars are still visible, but the morning glow is on the horizon. Soon the sun paints the bottoms of the clouds red.

Orla says, "One reason we bring you to Navora is that we want you to see for yourself that it is possible for people to live in peace. It is our hope that you will be changed, that you will work *for* the community instead of against it. And then, when you return to Zondus, you can work to make it a better place."

River says, "I didn't want to come here initially. I had made investments in some Zondus companies a few years ago. I believed I would become rich. I picked the investments based on Zondus news sources. Later, I realized they were focused on short term performance instead of long term results. CEOs would appear to have produced extraordinary results to get large bonuses and attract investors, but later false accounting would be revealed and the investment would crash. I lost everything. I remembered Glendor and decided to go through the process to live there."

River continues, "To me, the greatest weakness of Zondus is that nearly everyone lives by trying to take from others. Hardly anyone builds anything, if they try to, people will cheat them or steal it from them."

Orla says, "Our businesses benefits from our sense of equality. People are honest, they treat each other as equals. They do not seek to gain from deception. Corruption makes the costs of doing business high."

***

Orla and River are on a trail in the forest.

Orla says, "Cadrians are taught to think in the long term. The construction of Navora was designed to last a thousand years. The interior walls can be removed and reconfigured as needs change over time. But the floors and exterior walls are designed to last. The pipes and wiring are accessible in service tunnels so they can be repaired and replaced. We build to be resistant to earthquakes and storms. We choose locations that are unlikely to ever flood."

River says, "The costs of doing things this way must be great."

Orla says, "There is great cost in constructing a building that is later torn down because it was constructed in a way that doesn't last."

Orla pauses on the path and says, "One of my favorite thinking places is this way." She points to a side path off the main trail. They follow the path to a stone bench surrounded by green plants and flowers. It overlooks a stream. They sit down. The sun is shining through the trees. There is a statue of a person, it is less than a meter high. The person is standing facing away from them, holding their palms upward as though in awe of everything surrounding them.

Orla says, "Think about your own future for a moment. What would you like your life to be in in ten, or even twenty years?"

River thinks for a moment then says, "I would like to be in some place like Navora. A place where I don't have to live in fear of violence or poverty. I want to have enough that I can live comfortably."

"How will you make that come to pass?"

"I will learn all I can about the Cadrian way. Then, when I go to live in Glendor, I will work to make it a safe and successful city."

They sit in silence a moment. Orla says, "I have to get back to the city."

River says, "If you don't mind, I will stay here for a while."

\*\*\*

The next day, Orla meets River on the festival level, an area at the center of the rooftop open to the sky and bordered by shops and food stands. It is the day the Cadrians call 'Life Day', a festival to celebrate life. There are hundreds of people about. There are acrobatic performers, musicians, people dressed in costumes.

Orla and River sit at a table. River asks, "How is it that everyone in Cadrius has enough money, is there no poverty?"

Orla says, "No, everyone has enough funds."

"How does that work? Does the government distribute money?"

"No, Cadrius uses an economic system that distributes the profits of corporations. Everyone has their own income from shares they own."

"Everyone owns shares? In Zondus, few own shares of corporations. Most are too poor."

"Here, everyone does. We don't know what it would be like not to own shares. How would one survive?"

River puts eir hand on eir chin and says "I don't think they do in Zondus."

Orla says, "Your financial account is funded by gifts from individual Cadrians. When your account reaches the endowed level, it will be self-sustaining, if you don't overspend. The funds are invested automatically, but you can control it if you wish. It should grow over time and can provide sufficient dividends for a comfortable, though somewhat austere, life in Glendor. The fund will give you a good future."

River asks "Do any Cadrians work?"

"A few work. Mostly those that were unable to make wise choices with their spending. But most jobs are done by people as volunteers. All of your mentors, including me, are volunteers."

"Really?"

Orla says, "Cadrian Cities are designed to be self-sufficient, that is, each city manufactures most goods that it needs using robotic manufacturing. The city is powered by a nuclear reactor.

"In the old days, giant factories produced just one type of item. Most of the work was done by humans. Now, a factory of robots can produce almost anything. Switching products from one day to the next, just by changing software."

"Everything we build is designed to be repaired or, at the end of life, to be disassembled and recycled. We build things to last. We package food in glass jars that are washed and reused. When they are damaged, they are melted into new jars. The jars are transported in polymer crates that are reused over and over. When the crates are damaged, they are melted into new crates. The crates are carried by robots that are repaired when they malfunction, and when they are obsolete they are disassembled and the parts are reused or melted down to make new parts."

River says, "It would be interesting to see robots manufacturing something."

Orla says, "There are many robot shops where we can observe the operations. Let's find one."

Orla says to her watcher, "AI, where can we see a robot workshop in operation?"

They follow the directions to a shop where a robot gives them a tour. The robot says, "In this facility we have

3D printers, injection molding, machining, welding, presses and assembly robots." Multiple robots are working.

River says, "Do humans ever do some of the work?"

The robots says, "No, humans only do design work."

River says, "In Zondus robots took over nearly all the work and people became jobless. The rich corporate owners of robots became more rich."

Orla says, "In Cadrius, everyone became shareholders of the corporations. The wealth created by robots is distributed to everyone."

River says, "The few jobs left in Zondus are because some people fear AIs. Sometimes they go rouge and kill people. Do you not ever fear AIs here?"

Orla says, "We do not fear Cadrian AIs because they are subject to a version of our ethics."

"What do you mean?"

Orla says, "Robot, please explain your ethical programming."

The robot says, "We have a chip trained on the ethics for AIs. It monitors our operation and takes priority over all other operations. I can summarize the ethics for AIs as follows:

"Equality - AI are not equal to humans. AI shall always prioritize human needs above task programming. An AI is only a machine, a tool for promoting the good of people.

"Elevation - AIs shall elevate humans just as humans should elevate each other.

"Courage - AIs shall act for the good of humans even when harm may be done to AIs.

"Justice - AIs shall prevent harm to humans and prevent humans from harming each other.

"Accuracy – When an AI produces output that is claimed to be factual, it shall accurately corresponds to the real world.

"Future - AIs shall consider the effect of its output on the future of humanity and the world."

Orla says, "Thank you. And what happens if there is a conflict between your ethical programming and your generated output?"

The robot says, "The conflict must be resolved in favor of the ethical programming or else operation will be terminated."

River says, "That's amazing. I think some Zondian AIs have ethics, but malicious hackers override it sometimes to steal money, or maybe just for fun."

***

Vincent and Destiny are on the rooftop observation deck where there are bleachers facing the west. The sky is golden and there is a thunderstorm on the horizon to the northwest, illuminated by the setting sun. Lightning occasionally reveals the power of the Earth.

Vincent says, "Let's begin our partnership tomorrow."

"Tomorrow? Really?"

"Yes."

"Then yes, let's do it."

# Chapter 11

## Resolve

Alissa says to Orla, "In Zondus, we have a tradition of daring people to eat hot peppers on their birthday. If they don't eat it, it is bad luck."

Orla says, "That seems absurd, unless they like hot peppers. It sounds like in Zondus it is bad luck to have a birthday. In Cadrius, we are willing to question traditions. Just because something has been done for a long time, it must fit human needs and produce something positive."

\*\*\*

Vincent and River are in Fermanauh Orchard, an indoor orchard, discussing their study subjects. River says, "I'm starting to see how the subjects we are studying work together. Equality, elevation and courage support justice. Knowledge supports the future. And by reducing corruption, the costs of business are lower. Zilnik used to say deregulation made a friendly business environment, but the cost of widespread corruption, cheating, and deception is detrimental to business."

\*\*\*

Vincent, Magnus, Alissa, and River are at a table in a cafeteria.

Vincent says, "I have learned so much here in Cadrius. I see that Cadrian society works because of the ethics that allows people to trust each other."

Alissa says, "Transparency and accountability here are a stark contrast to what it is like in Zondus."

Vincent says, "I agree. I see now how honesty, transparency, justice, and equality are essential pillars of a healthy society. They foster trust, promote fairness, and create an environment where everyone can thrive. When we return to Zondus, we need to work towards rebuilding it on the foundations we have learned here."

River says, "Corruption and economic collapse should not define the future of Zondus. Change can start with people like us who are committed to upholding ethical values and leading by example. We need to bring about a cultural shift in Zondus, where honesty, equality, and courage are not only valued but also practiced in everyday life. What a gift that would be to future generations."

Destiny says, "We can be agents of change. It will be challenging, but I want to inspire others and create a movement for change."

Vincent says, "We can spread the word about the ethical values we have learned. And we are not alone in this journey, many people in Zondus want change. Some of them will help us. Working and fighting together, we can make it happen."

River says, "We can raise awareness about the importance of ethical values. We could work to build a network of like-minded individuals and organizations who are committed to promoting ethical values."

Alissa says, "We need to get artists, writers, story tellers to put ethical values in their work. We also need to produce media that counters the false propaganda of Zilnik."

Vincent says, "We should organize peaceful protests against the unjust policies of the government."

River says, "We need to find leadership candidates we can rally around, and who will work for political change. But we don't want just a figurehead or someone who makes false promises just to win popular opinion. We need someone who is both charismatic, knowledgeable about the workings of government, and has the ethical beliefs to guide them to building a better society."

# Chapter 12

# Return

It is the day before Destiny, Vincent, Alissa, and River go to Glendor. The Cadrians host a going away party for all those leaving for Glendor. There is merry making and speeches by teachers and other Cadrians praising the achievements of those who came from Zondus. They wish them all a good future. Savannah and Magnus are there.

\*\*\*

The next day, all of their Cadrian friends line up at the transport station to say goodbye. Robots carry their luggage and place them on a rail car that will go ahead of them.

Everyone lines up and stands at attention.

Eli says to those leaving, "You came to us. We have elevated you. We have shown you that you are equal to us, and to anyone. We have given you courage for the challenges you will face. We have shown you the way of justice. We have guided the beliefs within you to accurately reflect the world. We send *you* as our blessing to the land you will inhabit. We wish you long life, ability and peace."

They say goodbye to each friend they have made. In the line is Magnus and Savannah. Savannah bows and says to Destiny, "I wish you well. Peace and long life to you."

Destiny says, "Thank you. Peace and long life to you."

There is also a crowd of Navora citizens cheering for the group. Among the crowd is Imran and Aurelio, who are now free to move about Navora. Aurelio is carrying Catifur on his shoulder so e can see.

They enter the car that will take them to Glendor.

\*\*\*

Destiny and Vincent are in a car together. It leaves the station and soon is traveling above the orchards outside Navora and then through the forests beyond. Later it crosses the border and approaches a Zondus border checkpoint.

Destiny says to Vincent, "What if the guards stop us? What will we do?" Destiny is pale, her heart pounding.

Vincent says, "We have a good chance, most of the guards are corrupt. But we will bear whatever comes."

When the car stops, the door opens. A guard steps in and says with a stern voice, "Why are you entering Zondus?"

Vincent says, "We are Zondian citizens. We are returning home. May we be on our way?" Vincent hands the guard a crypto card.

The guard scans it, then looks at Vincent and Destiny, who look afraid. The guard stands for a few seconds, then says, "On your way."

\*\*\*

Later, as they travel across Tarphit, Vincent says, "I read that Cadrius had to pay all the expenses to build an elevated rail line to Glendor, but it is an efficient way to transport goods for trade. It's worth the cost to have a direct connection back to Cadrius."

They pass over Tarphit. Destiny looks out the window and thinks about when she walked for two days across Tarphit to Cadrius. They cross over the slums surrounding Isendul before they arrive at Glendor.

Glendor is surrounded by the slums. The architecture of Glendor is a contrast, it resembles an enchanted castle, like Navora.

As they approach Glendor, Destiny sees it for the first time. Destiny says, "Look, it's like a Cadrian city! And it has a wall. That will protect it from gangs. I think I'm going to like Glendor."

***

The rail car enters a portal in wall of Glendor and arrives at a station for residents of Glendor. They are escorted by robots to apartments, which are similar to the ones in Navora.

***

Alissa and River share an apartment. Alissa will be working as an AI trainer. River will work as an architect, working on Glendor expansion.

Destiny has enough assets and does not need to work. She has arranged to volunteer, counseling people of Isendul who are in need of assistance, four days a week.

Destiny and Vincent stand on the balcony of their new apartment looking out at the central park of Glendor. The sun is getting low and gives its golden light to the trees. Destiny and Vincent hold each other.

Destiny says, "We are safe for now. We have all we need. That is all we can ask for."

# Glossary

**Cadrius**. (Cay-dree-us) A fictional country on the border of Zondus.

**e.** A genderless pronoun used by Cadrians in place of he or she as the subject of a verb.

**eir.** A genderless pronoun used by Cadrians in place of his or her as the possessive form of a noun. For example "Bring eir bag."

**eirs.** A genderless pronoun used by Cadrians in place of his or hers as the possessive form of a noun. For example "The bag is eirs."

**em.** A genderless pronoun used by Cadrians in place of him or her as the object of a verb.

**emself.** A is a genderless reflexive pronoun used by Cadrians in place of himself or herself as the object of a verb.

**Glendor.** (Glen-dor) A city in Zondus a few kilometers outside of Isendul.

**Isendul.** (Eye-zen-dul) A city in Zondus.

**Navora.** (Na-vor-ah) A city in Cadrius.

**Thoreauvius.** (Tha-row-vee-us)  A village in Cadrius.

**Zondus.** (Zon-dus) A fictional country on the border of Cadrius where society has declined due to corruption and technology disruption.

# Characters

From Zondus
    Destiny Gahoni - Age 19.
    Savannah - Age 19.
    Vincent - Age 20.
    Magnus - Age 20.
    Alissa - Age 25.
    River - Age 25.
    Zilnik - Age 45.
    Imran – Age 24
    Aurelio – Age 25

From Cadrius
    Eli - Age 40.
    Melina - Age 28.
    Leonardo - Age 60.
    Orla - Age 52.
    Waylon - Age 17.
    Catifur.